I0573035

Her Christmas Project

by

J. J. RANSON

The His & Hers Christmas Series
Book 2

This is a work of fiction. Names, characters, places, and incidents are either the product of the author's imagination or are used fictitiously, and any resemblance to actual persons living or dead, business establishments, events, or locales, is entirely coincidental.

Her Christmas Project

COPYRIGHT © 2025 by Julie J. Ranson

All rights reserved.

No part of this book may be used or reproduced in any manner whatsoever without written permission of the author or Painted Pen Press, LLC, except in the case of brief quotations embodied in critical articles or reviews. Any use of this publication to train generative artificial intelligence (AI) technologies to generate text is expressly prohibited.

Contact Information: jjransonauthor@gmail.com

Cover Art by Julie J. Ranson

Painted Pen Press, LLC, 7410 Hull Street Road, Ste 200, Unit #345, North Chesterfield, VA 23235

Publishing History First Edition, 2025

Trade Paperback ISBN 979-8-9990415-0-0

Digital ISBN 979-8-9990415-1-7

The His and Hers Christmas Series – Book 2

Published in the United States of America

Chapter 1

Angie

I slammed the car door and hit the lock button on my key-fob. The neighbor's black lab barked through the fence, and I cringed at the noise I was creating. The rest of the street remained Sunday-afternoon-quiet, except for the rustle of red and gold leaves in the soft breeze. A bright yellow oak leaf danced across my foot, mocking me with its happiness.

I don't normally slam doors, but my disastrous date had me rankled. Am I forgettable? Apparently, since Matt called me Amelia. Twice! On our second date! I growled as I tossed my coat onto the hall-tree. My brown eyes blazed in its center mirror; the etched glass framed my scowling face. What a picture.

The date did not go as planned. No, not at all.

I'd picked our meeting place for lunch. After meeting for a drink months ago, we agreed a longer date would help us get better acquainted. The Garden Bar's famous blue door opens into a palazzo-style room—terracotta tile floors provided a warm foundation for so many potted plants. When she finally gets back in town. I'd have to bring Sylvie here. My dearest friend is a plant nerd—weird, in my opinion — and she's got some mad gardening skills.

He's here. Matt. He and I had our first and only date back in early July. We liked each other enough to meet again—a sign of progress in my failure of a dating life. Actually, he invited me to a concert over Labor Day, but I already had plans. I supposed he may be the real deal. I didn't know what I wanted, and wondered again why I was trying to find the love of my life as the holidays approached. Didn't finding that perfect person require a bit more focus than I possessed? The idea of perfection raised a bunch of other questions I'd ponder later. Perhaps bring them up to Sylvie, my best friend.

Matt held up a hand in greeting as he approached the table. I'd picked one by the window when I arrived early, so I could watch people on the busy sidewalk outside. His brown hair tapered above his ears and the part on the left side was as straight as if an arrow had sliced through it.

I stood as soon as I saw him coming in the door.

"Amelia. Thanks for setting this up." Matt leaned in and brushed his cheek against mine. He smelled like wood and vanilla.

I stepped back. "Angie."

Matt's face was a study in confusion. "Oh. I'm so sorry. Angie." He said my name with emphasis, as though committing it to memory. I refrained from rolling my eyes. That would be as rude as forgetting a girl's name.

"No worries. I'm glad you were free. Sorry I was too slammed before."

"Glad you survived the summer. I get it."

He probably did get it. Matt worked for a trucking company, so he'd surely experienced the crazy flurry of busy-ness that several holidays crammed together can bring. Heading into the Hallo-Thanks-Mas days, my life was about to get too harried for words. Last year, I had to place my online dating profile on vacation to allow me to focus on the store's holiday craziness. Not fair at all. Would I ever have a real life? It's a question that started looming large when I turned thirty a couple of years ago.

Summer was over and it's "stuff the stockroom for three holidays" time. Displayed on the shelves behind the stockroom doors is a seasonal mix of earthy tones and the glossy jewel ones I especially love. Fun stuff for our customers, but not as much for the workers who had to get it to the floor displays. Dad has been grumbling about all the boxes, which is funny because he insists on approving all the purchases I make.

"Christmas will be insane, as I'm sure you are aware." I rolled my eyes as I placed a black cloth napkin on my lap.

"Ugh. I know what you mean. Sorry."

I waved away his sympathy.

"Enough about my business tragedies. How have you been?"

"Pretty good. Looking forward to closing out the year, seeing my family, the usual. Did you go on vacation this summer?"

"Nope. My best friend and I had hoped to do something, but she had the nerve to get engaged."

"Wow. Fun times, huh?"

"Stressed days. What about you?"

"One of my married coworkers rented a beach house on the gulf. All I managed was a long weekend."

So, we're both boring, I mused. I was rescued from saying that out loud when a cute blonde server named Chloe showed up with water for Matt. Mine was half full, so she topped it off out of a clear plastic pitcher, ice plopping into my glass as she poured.

"Can I share our specials?"

"Please," Matt said as he closed the menu.

We both ordered salads, mine with spicy shrimp and his with grilled salmon.

He chuckled as he commented, "We both must have some diet goals."

I nodded. "I should eat better most days."

"You definitely don't need to be on a weight loss plan."

I bristled at such a personal remark. Did he mean I was too skinny? Mind your business, Matt.

Silence, not entirely uncomfortable, slid into the vacant space above our little wooden table. I brushed my hands over my legs and smiled at Matt. I noticed his eyes were hazel and rimmed with thick, long lashes. Why do guys have the most gorgeous eyelashes?

Instead of talking, we sipped water and looked around the room. On our first date, we had chatted endlessly. Back then, we were kinda interviewing each other. Our online dating profiles on Flirtable only told so much about our lives. Clearly, the software believed we had a few things in common, and we'd decided to spend more get-to-know-you time, which had to mean something. Didn't it?

"Here ya go." Chloe the server stood beside our table with two square white plates, one in each hand.

In unison, he and I thanked her as she set our plates in front of us.

"This looks fantastic," Matt said.

"Mmm." Having skipped breakfast, I was already chewing a succulent shrimp.

"Hungry girl? I like that."

"I'm rarely shy about eating." I giggled as I used my fork to create a lettuce and cucumber combo.

"This place has an interesting vibe. Have you been before?"

I had been once in April with another guy I'd met online. Dave. The best part of that meeting was the location. I would not share the details with Matt. Well, unless we kept seeing each other, and then I could see myself telling him about my dating woes. He probably had some tales to tell, too.

"I've been once before. It is cool. I love the jazz."

"Haven't experienced much jazz music, but it sounds nice."

He thought it was nice? Jazz is awesome! My parents hardly played anything else at home, and the rhythms shifted my moods from melancholy to joy on a Sunday afternoon. I grew up nerdy, and perhaps a little confused, on the music front. Of course, I also love the music of my generation—pop music plays in my car and in my office at the store most days.

"What's your favorite music?"

"Um." Matt looked up to the right, thinking. Seriously? Maybe we should've covered this in July.

"I like a lot of bands. Like, um, rock and country."

"Okay." I nodded encouragingly, even though I was deeply concerned about having to teach a man about great tunes. What if I looked forward to the chance? Shouldn't I be more open to new things?

"So, what's your favorite radio station?"

"I usually listen to podcasts."

"Gotcha." We wouldn't be going out dancing, clearly.

Matt had the decency to squirm in his seat, because what interesting human had no radio favorites? While I dug around my salad, I kept one eye on him, knowing he was searching for a new, or shall we say, better, topic. I chewed and waited, while feeling a little mean about letting him hang out there.

The silence grew like dough rising on the stove. I was okay with it before, but it seemed like Matt was punishing me.

"So, Halloween is a couple weeks away. Got any plans?" Lord, I didn't ask that. I dipped my head and gave rapt attention to my shrimp.

Matt chuckled. "You're asking me out for Halloween?"

"Oh, heavens no." Realizing I was making bad things worse, my throat clenched. "Just making conversation."

I smiled brightly at Matt, and as I did, a small piece of lettuce got stuck in my throat. When clearing it didn't work, I tried to cough. Then I took a sip of water.

"Are you okay? You're turning pink."

I pointed to my neck and coughed. Another sip of water.

"Allow me." Matt left his seat and patted my back between the shoulder blades. I kept coughing. Finally, I felt the thing let loose and held up a hand.

"Thank you," I croaked out as he sat down. "I'm so embarrassed."

"Don't be. Could happen to anyone. Actually, one time, I was..." Matt started his story about choking on candy as a kid. I listened with one ear and played with my salad. I think I smiled and clucked in surprise at the right places as he spun the yarn.

He was quite handsome, and I enjoyed listening to his deep voice. What else could we talk about? Hobbies, books, movies?

"Well, since we're talking about choking, haha, what's your favorite food, Matt?"

"Hmm. That shouldn't be a tough question."

I caught myself about to roll my eyes. How can I get to know someone who doesn't know himself? What had we talked about the first time? He might have told me about being from Natchez, and I likely shared stories of growing up in Birmingham. Yeah, that seemed about right.

"Steak. I love me some ribeye!"

"I love steak too, but I probably enjoy seafood more."

"No wonder you picked this place. This salmon is tasty."

"Glad it's a hit. I have a girlfriend I want to bring here sometime. When she's back in town."

"Do you have a lot of friends you hang out with, Angie?"

I twirled my glass around its wet circle on the table. "Not really. I work so much. Friends get tired of you telling them you can't do something. They quit asking eventually."

"I'm a lucky guy then to have some of your time."

"I definitely need to work on my dat-, um, my social life."

"I hear ya. It's brutal out there." Matt shook his head.

I gave him my most sympathetic look. He was going to experience more brutality, as he put it, when I told him I didn't want to date him again. Or what if I dragged out the time until we'd both moved on? Sigh. That sounded awful. I'm just like my friend: clueless about dating and romance. I sure gave her a ton of advice last year, as if I had some expertise.

My phone buzzed, and I looked down at my purse sitting on the floor. I glanced back at Matt, who was attentive to what I'd do next.

"Do you need to answer that?" He sounded suspicious, as though he suspected I'd planned to get called away.

"Nope. It's Sunday lunchtime. My folks are at brunch with friends. Can't think of anyone else who'd call me."

Matt looked relieved. "Cool. I thought you were going to bolt on me."

I giggled. "No, that's definitely not my style. I don't play games." I don't, right? But what had I just been thinking about stringing him along rather than being honest about our dating future? I wasn't about to deal with that ugly truth then.

He reached for my hand. "I'd like to see you again. That you asked me to lunch means a lot after we let other things get in the way."

I blushed and mumbled, "Sure." What else was I supposed to say?

In a blessed moment, Chloe showed up with the check on a little black plastic tray. I grabbed it while Matt protested intensely.

"This was my invitation, remember?"

"Right."

"And it's the twenty-first century," I whispered gravely across the table.

"Ha ha. You're hilarious."

As I poked around my purse for my wallet, I saw Sylvie was the one who'd called me. For a dating update, for sure. I'd call her when I got home.

Matt walked me to my car, which was parked a block away. I opened the car door to put it between us. I really, really didn't want him to kiss me. I feared he might, since he'd already brushed my cheek when he arrived at the restaurant.

"I'm glad we did this," I said, holding a hand up above my eyes to shield the blinding autumn sun.

"Absolutely. Hope we can do it again."

I nodded and smiled as I slid into the driver's seat.

"Why am I not surprised that you drive a little red car?"

"Girl's gotta have fun!"

He backed away as I started it up. Relief flowed down my body. I'd been holding myself taut for two hours.

I saw his lips move, and I'm pretty sure he said, "Bye, Amelia."

Good grief. I gritted my teeth and drove off.

Chapter 2

Angie

"Okay, let's hear it."

"That's how you answer the phone now, Sylvie?" I poked out my bottom lip and blew air upward into my bangs. They're getting too long, but I hadn't taken scissors to them yet while I contemplated letting them grow.

"Just channeling you, my friend. You're the busiest-body-est friend I have."

"Who's making up words?" I laughed as I poured my usual Sunday wine.

"How was the repeat performance?"

"Eh."

"What happened?"

"I liked him a few months ago and wanted to learn more about him. And that's exactly why I said, 'eh.' It was more than disappointing."

"Ugh. Sorry."

I shrugged as I walked into my bedroom at my parents' house, where I've lived my entire life and hadn't gotten up the nerve to move out. Sometimes I feel a little stupid and behind the times whenever I catch a glimpse of whatever life updates my old classmates share on social media. I bet I had more savings than they do. So there's that.

"Sylvie, he doesn't have a favorite radio station. And..."

"And?"

"He had to actually think about his favorite food!"

"Gosh, he couldn't get over some pretty low bars. That's too bad."

"Yes, it is. The worst part--"

"Yeah?"

"He called me 'Amelia.' Twice!"

"What? That's just--"

"Awful. Pathetic. There's something wrong with me." Tossing back the last drops of red wine, I headed downstairs for more.

"You stop right there, little lady. There's nothin' wrong with you."

In her sigh, I heard the weight of frustration with men and her love for me. We'd been through a lot since middle school. Sylvie is the one who told me about the Flirtable dating site, but she made it through only three dates. Then she met Pete. But he wasn't one of her online matches. Long story. They're so cute together and I witnessed that firsthand because she brought him to Alabama right after New Year's Day. Then they got engaged on Valentine's Day. Another woman in my age group bites the dust and I'm still floundering like a... like a daggone fish on the beach.

"Enough about my horrible love life. Have you and Pete settled into a routine since he's back in Richmond?"

"Routine? Uh, maybe. I dunno. We're too busy with work to see each other all the time. He is on a tight deadline for his next book and the movie script he's been asked to review. We talk or text every day. We hang out on the weekends. And he's so sweet. I'm spoiled. He just told me he made me a mani-pedi appointment for next week. A birthday gift."

"Awww, that is too sweet. Can we talk about the wedding plans? Are you only coming down here for the shower and then back for the wedding? I want more time with my friend. Just us time. The shower is in only three weeks."

"What's wrong? Can I help? Did you talk to Momma?"

"Whoa. Nothing's wrong. I'm relieved your momma got me the country club and its catering. My main assignments are the decorations and managing the guest list. And your dear sister is coming early to help me."

"Phew. As for our girl time, I wish. Having the shower and wedding during the holidays is a bit much. For all involved. Pete and I are putting a lot of strain on family with our Christmas wedding wish."

"I'm sorry to ask for more with all you have on your plate. Just wish you could stay an extra day after the shower."

"Don't apologize, Ang, it's a fair complaint. I sure appreciate the love." Sylvie giggled. As if she needed extra love. But at least she knows that friend love is special, and ours is one-of-a-kind.

"I've forgotten to ask about your wedding venue. You were trying to squeeze into that modern spot downtown. What's it called?"

"The Main Center."

"I'm shocked your momma didn't make you get hitched at the Baptist church you grew up in."

"Yeah, well, no drinking, no dancing, equals no wedding."

I laughed.

"Priorities!"

"Yup," Sylvie replied with a laugh.

"So you got it? For Sunday the twenty-second, like you wanted?"

"We did! Sunday afternoon was an easier request for them so late in the game."

"I'm thrilled for you. I drove past it the other day. It's very shiny."

"Shiny? What do you mean?"

"Nothing negative. I just meant it's very modern and glossy. I can see you getting married there."

"I'm so glad you approve, maid of honor! It's a stunning place. My dress is perfect for it."

Sylvie had come back to Birmingham in July to dress shop. She spent an entire week with her parents and they 'bout near drove her mad. She stayed over two nights with me to get away from them.

The dress she picked is a column of white matte satin with a draped cowl in the back. It shows her curves perfectly. The dresses her sister and I will wear are such a dark red, we look like delicious glasses of Cabernet. I fell in love with the lace bodice and was the ultimate salesgirl for that choice. Every wedding needs lace, in my opinion, and Sylvie's dress doesn't have a bit of it, so the maid and matron of honor are fulfilling that requirement.

"Hey, tell me about Pete and your parents. I mean, they still love him, right? It was a thrilling surprise, but is it still great?"

"So, my Daddy...turns out he has a bookshelf filled with all of Pete's books! Go figure."

"Win-win, my friend."

"They are still completely sold. Lots of fandom going on to this day. Daddy would like to chat regularly with Pete. I never thought he'd wanted a son, but now I wonder."

My dearest friend in the whole world heaved a sigh bigger than the ones she'd breathed while figuring out if Pete was "the one" ten months ago.

I stayed quiet, processing all the romantic activity going on in my best friend's life. When would it be my turn? Would I ever get a turn? I'd been having serious doubts for so long, and my recent dating experiences have raised my fears nearly to distraught level.

Sylvie sighed again, and I sighed with her.

"Does your momma know you're out dating up a storm?" she asked, as if she'd read my tortured mind.

"A storm? That's reaching. I told her that I'm trying to get out there and meet someone. Since I live at home, I try to share some things with the parents. And, of course, Mom is both happy and worried. We cannot avoid our mothers and their convoluted thinking about the world of how dating should be."

"Whatever is she worried about?"

"Oh, I dunno. That I'll get hurt. Emotionally and physically. Online dating sounds dangerous to her. Dad seems cool with it. Did I ever tell you that they met through a matchmaker?" I bit the inside of my lip as I pondered Dad's view on his only child, a daughter, spending time with the opposite sex.

"What? That's incredible. I love it! What a story to have."

"Yeah, I think it's cool. I've convinced myself that's why Dad doesn't think online dating is weird. I wish Mom wasn't such a downer about it sometimes."

"She must know you'll be careful. But let's face it, we cannot control what happens to our hearts."

I stayed quiet, pondering her new experience with love. She sure couldn't control how Pete touched her heart. I'd only pretended to be an expert to help her.

"Where'd you go, Angie?"

"Thinking about hearts."

"Ah, yes. Things can get out of control real fast, my friend."

"I noticed."

"But I've kept you long enough. Since this is your only day off, I better let you go do laundry or whatever."

"Thanks, friend. I'm so glad you called."

"Good luck on your dates this week. Don't forget, I'll need updates. Call or text any time!"

"Yes, ma'am. Talk soon."

After we hung up, I gathered up the clothes hanging off my closet doorknobs and scattered on the floor, tossing them into my ancient white wicker laundry basket. My folks had come home while Sylvie and I chatted, so I drifted down with my laundry expecting to have to catch up on dating news with at least one of them.

"Hey Mom. How was brunch?"

Mom stood up from bending over the oven door. "It was nice, dear. The Howletts said to tell you 'Hi'."

"Hi back. I'm doing laundry. Got anything to go in?"

She shook her head as she washed her hands at the sink. "Your father did ours yesterday."

I shook my head at the sheer luck of my mom. Perhaps I'd start asking my dates about their household chore philosophy.

As if she read my mind, Mom asked, "How was your lunch date, honey?"

I scrunched up my face and shrugged. "Fine."

"That's not an endorsement. What happened? Did he do something bad?"

What she meant by "something bad" was anybody's guess, and I really didn't want to know, so I shook my head. I wasn't about to tell her he called me by the wrong name twice—too humiliating. "It was just so-so. No big deal."

"I've no doubt you know what you're doing. And... for what it's worth, darling girl, the heart always knows." She patted me on the shoulder while I dropped my clothes into the washer.

"Thanks, Mom. I'll figure it out."

"Of course. I have faith that one day I will have grandchildren."

Exasperated, I groaned out loud, "Mom!"

She had the good grace to giggle as she left to join my dad in the living room, where he was watching football. From the kitchen, the murmur of their voices carried their affection and decades of history. My shoulders slumped from the weight of the loneliness that had sidled onto them. The people I loved most—my parents and Sylvie—were happier than pigs in mud.

I felt so lost and alone all of a sudden. I needed some mud, it seemed.

After the failed lunch with Matt, I was desperate to improve the odds for my future dates, but lacked the confidence I'd pull it off. And honestly, only one date had to go well, right? It's embarrassing to think in such terms. So foolish. I had something to offer a man, but it's possible he'd have to tell me what that was. My self-worth wasn't trading very high. I surely don't qualify as a runway model with my petite build, dark curls, and brown eyes.

When I connected with the guys on Flirtable, I feared too much time wasting on the front end. I'd limited Jake to a coffee date and Brian to a drink at the bar around the corner from the store.

Jake arrived late, but he ran into the coffeehouse with his hands flying through his shaggy, dark blond dreadlocks. Yet again I got there first, so I stood at the table, so he'd see me and figure out I was his online match. He approached, uttering profuse apologies. He was kind of adorable if you're into a messy, just-rolled-out-of-bed style, and he actually had a tan. I found myself charmed. He was a surprise, a pleasant one. Since he managed a restaurant, we shared some good laughs about customers, managing people, and how our work might limit our staying connected. Restaurant and retail life are very similar in time commitment and stress levels. Two hours later, we both looked at our watches and gasped.

"Oops," I said. "Late for work. You?"

"Not yet. I'm working the dinner shift tonight."

"Well, Jake, this was fun. Thank you for winking at me online." I gave him my sassiest smile, but avoided batting my eyelashes, which would likely send mascara flakes under a contact lens.

"Hey, let's try again. I'm sorry it took a while to get this scheduled."

"No worries. We did it and it was fun."

As we stood, he motioned for me to go first to the stained-glass door leading outside, where I was blinded by a fall morning sunshine that washed over us like white dust. The coffeehouse only had small windows up front, so it'd been rather dim. A fireplace had made it toasty inside, and the strange October chill in the air forced me to pull up my sweater collar around my ears. Jake rubbed his hands together while he faced me with a big smile on his cute, tanned face. I couldn't get over his tan, but didn't find the nerve to ask about it.

"Hey, I really wanna see you again. Is it possible we can get ourselves together easier next time? Now that we've met in person."

I smiled up at him and nodded. "I'd love that." And I meant it. We headed in opposite directions on that sidewalk. I peeked over my shoulder, hoping he'd be looking back too, but he was striding quickly away, hands in his jacket pockets. I got to work in just a few minutes as vehicle traffic was surprisingly light, glad I hadn't had enough time to dissect our goodbye.

Vanessa found me humming to smooth jazz in my office an hour later. She leaned on the doorjamb and grinned. "Someone had a good coffee date."

I shrugged. "It went well, I guess."

"Seeing him again?"

"Most likely."

She turned back to the store, tossing a reminder over her shoulder, "We're almost out of those new chocolates. Better order some more."

"On it."

But I didn't hop right on that chore, instead I rested my chin in my hand and stared out the office window, which looked out onto Maple Road. My family's store is just off Woodward in the city's old shopping district. We're friends with folks in nearly all the stores and restaurants around us, and together we've fought against "dumb" initiatives driven by local politicians. To say we're like family would be an understatement. My parents started counting on the support of other business owners long before I was born.

My great-grandparents had opened a dry goods store in this same spot in the early 1900s when immigrants from Sicily found their way to Alabama. Strange, I know. But they were the first Caruso family to settle in this state. The store passed to my grandparents, and they changed the look and feel. Then Dad had the vision to gobble up adjacent properties whenever he had the chance. By the time I was a teenager, Magic City Mercantile was triple the size of the original dry goods store. Magic City is a nickname for my hometown from way back when my great-grands came to America. Dad changed the name of the store once it occupied half the block. He'd "made his own magic" is what he told me when the front counter met level with my eyes. The store held—and still holds—a special sort of magic for me. I can't imagine doing anything else. Well, most days. Honestly, sometimes I feel a bit shackled to this entire block of buildings.

When I graduated from Birmingham-Southern College ten years ago, I got our entire inventory online. When he turned sixty, Dad reduced his hours to about thirty a week. My office used to be Mom's, but she didn't come to the store much anymore, except when I took a rare vacation. Dad worked Monday through Friday from about ten until four. Basically, they're both semi-retired.

Mom got super involved in volunteerism, and her hours started diminishing when I returned to the shop after college. It was a given, period, that their only daughter would keep the store open forever. Where else would I go, anyway? Who'd have me with my limited experience?

Dad mostly worked on inventory issues like returning damaged goods and keeping the backroom in good order. Basically, he spent most of his time with a box-cutter in his hand. He's only sixty-five, healthy, and I hoped the Caruso's longevity gene extended to my father as well. I'd like him to keep working for a while longer so I can get the staffing perfect before he retires. Vanessa is the assistant manager, and I love, love, love her.

When Dad left the shop for good, it'd be me, Vanessa, and two part-time students in either high school or college, meaning a constant revolving door of retail trainees. I'd talked to my father about hiring someone to train in the stockroom with him, but he'd been a little cheap on that front. He and Mom would probably use the word "reticent," but I maintained he was being stubborn and unreasonable. That he never complained at Christmas and inventory seasons was remarkable because I sure did complain. A lot.

The sounds of the bell chiming and Vanessa's customer greeting drew my gaze away from the street and back to my messy desk, covered with packing slips and notes on pages ripped from a yellow legal pad, in Dad's handwriting. I wish we had a more efficient way for me to compare invoices and his comments on the return forms. I sighed as I woke the sleeping computer and began matching invoices to the mess of paperwork that had accumulated since Labor Day.

My lonely heart wanted me to check my Flirtable account, in case Jake had messaged me. Worrying about my dating life would have to wait.

Chapter 3

Brian

THE MAHOGANY BAR HAD a gloss that rivaled a freshly waxed car in the sunshine. It ran the depth of the first half of The Bistro in Magic City. It curved in front so anyone sitting on the curve had a full view of the restaurant, with their back to the windows and the sidewalk. That's where I perched, because I could also see the door. I prefer facing the door in a public place, so I got to the bar early.

I'm a little hungry after working all day, but my blind date, Angie, wanted to meet for just a drink. I get it. A sit-down dinner with a stranger is a huge commitment of time and energy, so I agreed without blinking an eye.

She's an attractive woman, assuming she looks like her profile picture on Flirtable. Believe me, pictures can lie. Or it's the poster who lies by omission or bad timing—you know, like using a photo from ten years ago? I've had a few disappointments, and I suppose it's conceivable that I also haven't met someone's expectations.

Don't get me wrong, looks are not everything. I honestly believe in chemistry and it's my deepest desire to meet the woman of my dreams. One who'll make me smile any time she crosses my mind, and makes me laugh when we're together. My belief in the mutual power of laughter and love came from a lifetime with my so-in-love parents. Being a squishy romantic will always remain a well-guarded secret around my guy friends. No one needs that kind of grief.

Spinning my glass on the slick bar, I'd gotten lost in thoughts of my dream woman. Then, I noted her arrival. Stuck between the exterior and interior doors, she shook her long hair and fluffed the top of her head. I think she checked her lipstick in the stained-glass mirror in the vestibule. I didn't recall her hair being curly in the photo. "Here we go again" was my initial disappointed reaction.

She smiled at the hostess and pointed at me. I stood and waved when she came through the second set of doors. I studied her as she navigated past some tables, unsure if she was avoiding looking at me or if she had a sincere curiosity about the place as her gaze flitted across tables. As she approached, she looked up at me and offered a gorgeous smile, then stuck out her right hand.

"Pleasure to meet you, Brian."

"Thank you for coming."

As she slid up onto the red leather bar seat, I asked, "You ever been here?"

"Once, which is surprising since it's three blocks from work! Crazy, huh?"

Oh, she was cute with that curly dark hair and round brown eyes. Angie was so tiny, I immediately felt protective.

"Is it okay to sit here at the bar? You don't mind?"

"It's fine. Good view of the place and all the people. You like people-watching?"

I nodded and took a sip of my drink. The ice clattered around, reminding me to signal the bartender.

"Where are my manners? What're you having, Angie?"

She pursed her rosy lips, so I watched her while she studied the colorful backdrop of liquor bottles. "It's like stained glass, isn't it?"

"Mm. Indeed."

The bartender, Gary, laid down a cocktail napkin and said, "What'll it be?"

"How 'bout a gin and tonic?"

Gary slapped the bar and turned to the well for the gin. He held up a dark green bottle and raised his eyebrows. Angie gave him a thumbs up.

"What are you drinking?"

"Vodka tonic. Simple, like me." I smirked.

"Your profile didn't make you sound simple at all. Hiking, swimming, paddle-boarding." She ticked the activities off on her fingers. Long, narrow tapers polished in deep pink. That minuscule dash of surprise about her hair slipped away. Her hair sparkled with the misty rain that began falling right after I got here, reminding me of the rhinestone hairpins a prom date had worn so long ago, and I wondered if everything about her had that same shine.

Angie had said she'd come straight from work, but she looked fresh as a daisy in black jeans and black and white checked blazer. We kinda matched, as I'd worn a black blazer with my khakis to work. She was the brighter spot with that gorgeous smile plus the deep orange blouse. I wondered if she'd chosen it because Halloween was only a week away. I reckoned it might help sell more goods if one dressed for the holiday.

"What do you do for fun, Angie?"

"Hmm. I often work six days a week. Sunday is my only day off. I do laundry, read, and go out with girlfriends now and then. I don't have much fun, to be honest."

"Perhaps I can help with that." I took a sip and saw wariness and, possibly, doubt playing across her face. I'd been too bold too soon, I worried. One day at a time, a phrase my brother John recited often after finishing his recovery program. One minute at a time was more like it in the dating world.

She twirled her glass on the bar, the wet ring under it growing as she worked it.

"I'm kinda hungry, are you?"

Wow. She likes me. At least a little.

"When I grumbled about having a late dinner, my work team's administrative assistant, Marcia, offered me a protein bar. But, yeah, I can definitely eat."

"Should we ask for a table here?"

"Let me check." I headed to the hostess station to get us on the list. Seven o'clock wasn't too late for dinner and that protein bar... it was gone. What a surprising night — I was having dinner with a beautiful woman.

"Thank you," Angie said as I held her chair at a back corner table. I couldn't believe we'd been given prime seating by a window and away from the kitchen. What a lucky night! I caught a whiff of something floral as I stood behind her and I started to lose myself in what-could-be's. I get carried away too fast, I admit. But she was something, for sure.

Angie quickly buried herself in the menu, so I did the same. I couldn't help observing her as she flipped from the front to the back, obviously having a food selection debate inside her head. I decided to help her out.

"Would you like to share an appetizer to get us started? I mean, if you need more time to consider your dinner options."

She shook her head. "I'm not much of an appetizer person. It would ruin my dinner. How do you think I maintain this girlish figure?"

I laughed, and she giggled. Girlish figure indeed.

"I was always a little chunky through middle and high school. It took a college commute and working at the store to drop my weight. Instead of gaining the freshman fifteen, I lost fifteen pounds during my first year of college. Oh boy, maybe that's too much information on a first date?"

She brushed a curl off her forehead for about the hundredth time. Might be a nervous tic. A cute one at that. I liked seeing those bright fingernails flashing through her dark hair.

"Well, if we're confessing, I owe you one."

"No, you absolutely do not."

I held up a hand. Fair's fair. We were getting to know each other. Why not dig a little deep? I already knew I would ask her out again.

"I used to wear a size triple-x shirt."

"You did not." She glanced over my arms and upper body, then returned her gaze to my face.

"I sure did, back in middle school. So, where'd you go to school?"

"Here. Birmingham High School, then I studied business at Birmingham-Southern College. I've never lived anywhere else. What about you?"

"Tuscaloosa born and raised. Like you, I stayed at home for college. Saved my parents some money, especially since I'm the youngest. Not much tuition money left."

"My friend, Sylvie, went to Alabama in Tuscaloosa! You could've met."

The server appeared with glasses of water and an electronic pad in his hand.

"Oops, are we ready to order? I've decided on something."

"Go ahead."

While I pretended to study the menu, I listened to Angie ask polite questions about the steak salad, and substitute the dressing offered. She ordered a glass of Merlot. I admired the soft beauty of her brown eyes, which conveyed an honesty and openness I wouldn't take for granted.

I ordered a second vodka tonic and the same salad. A guy needs to maintain his own figure, and though mine was anything but girlish, at thirty-four I'd noticed recent evidence of excess food and drink. I'd been committed to watching my waistline for the last five years, hence the constant weekend activity.

After the server left, promising our food would be up shortly, I followed up on her friend's college path. Turned out I graduated two years ahead of her with a Civil Engineering degree. As a business major, Angie's friend would have been an unlikely classmate.

"If I meet her one day, I'm sure we'd share at least a few similar college memories." What the heck was I thinking? First dates weren't supposed to go like this, with me all up in her life like we're a couple.

"Yeah. I suppose that's true." Angie cast her gaze around to the nearby tables, avoiding eye contact with me. I could be such an idiot, mentally kicking myself for being so brazen.

"Sorry. I'm assuming things not in evidence. As they say in the courtroom shows I watch," I offered, hoping she'd understand my self-mockery.

"I can see us going out again."

I breathed a dramatic sigh of relief. "Really? Thank you. I heard myself sounding a little creepy there."

She giggled again, the friendliness of it brushing over my heart. And for the second time in one night, she had initiated the idea of more togetherness. I'd never forget that Angie suggested we stay on for dinner, like she'd read my mind.

The scent of charred beef assailed me as our server slid a salad plate in front of each of us.

"Yum-o," said Angie, a grin splitting her face as she picked up the steak knife on the plate and started cutting. The crunch of lettuce filled the small space between us. The intimacy of the corner and small table lent the idea that we might bump heads as we bent over our meal. Outside, the street and sidewalk glistened with rain, the glass streaked with rivulets of water that couldn't stop their race to the sill.

I didn't mind this silence at all, another strange feeling for a guy who grew up in a loud home with chatter-filled dinner hours. I tended to fill silences with a story whenever the quiet fogged up the atmosphere; silence is almost always palpable to me and it makes me a little nervous, I suppose.

Angie stared at me over her wine glass. "Cheers to blind dates," she said as she raised her glass toward me. I lifted my glass in salute.

"Cheers to Flirtable."

"I dunno about that. Not completely." She shook her head.

"Bad experiences?"

"Not for me. My friend, Sylvie… um, she had a couple of mishaps, which almost convinced me to give up before I gave it a chance. She's since met someone offline and is happier than a bug in a rug."

"So we have some things in common, like we attended college where we grew up. What else, I wonder. I'm the youngest of three, all boys."

"I am an only child." She rolled her eyes.

"Why'd you roll your eyes?"

"Oh, you know, people have all kinds of negative notions about the only child."

"My best friend in college was an only child, and she was such a cool person. She never came across as spoiled or whatever."

A flicker of something crossed Angie's face, but what I couldn't tell. I shouldn't have said the word spoiled, I guessed. Instead of filling in the quiet space between us, I waited to see if she'd share her thoughts.

"Your best friend was a girl?"

"Yeah, Maggie. We both majored in civil engineering and the male-to-female ratio was about five to one. I don't know if you're aware of this, but college guys aren't always kind."

"Ha-ha. For real." She slowly spun her empty wine-glass on the table, a depressing sign that our night would eventually end. Too soon for me.

"I befriended her, and we studied together. She didn't need a tutor, of course, but we got close over our textbooks and fancy calculators. Maggie was probably the best friend I ever had."

Angie frowned. "Was?"

I shook my head. "Nothing like marriage and a new city to break up a friendship. Especially between a guy and girl. Her husband wasn't too keen on me walking her down the aisle, but she'd lost both her parents during middle school. She stood her ground with him. Still, we don't talk much nowadays. Just the occasional text message."

"How sad! I can't imagine. Poor thing."

"Didn't mean to be a downer. How 'bout we discuss next time?"

"Okay."

"What're you doing this weekend?"

She laughed. I did it again. Did she think I was rushing things?

"What do you have in mind? I work until at least four most Saturdays, unless I plan way ahead for a day off."

"My hiking group has an outing on Sunday. It starts at ten. Will that mess with your schedule, like church or anything?"

"Church? I haven't been to St. Ann's for years. I started drifting away after my confirmation."

"Your family's Catholic? I was raised Methodist. And we have in common our lack of attendance."

"When you work six days a week, Sundays get busy real fast. With things other than church."

"You haven't answered about going hiking with me."

"Do I need special clothes or shoes?"

"Absolutely not. But given it's late October and we'll be in the shade most of the time, a hat and scarf are recommended. A jacket, at the least." I grinned at her.

"No duh."

"So we're on?"

"Tell me where to be."

"Parking can be sketchy at the trailhead, so how about we meet somewhere and then carpool?"

"Works for me."

"Do you want to keep messaging in Flirtable or switch to cell phones?" I crossed my fingers under the table.

Angie pulled out her cell phone and asked, "What's your number? I'll text you, so you have mine."

I flushed with the pleasure of having her number in my possession. I'd failed at keeping my hopes in check—Angie had made my day.

Chapter 4

Angie

I DROVE HOME IN the rain, hoping to catch Sylvie before she went to bed. The storm lashing against my windshield prevented me from calling her in the car. Safety first, my dad's mantra. Well, that and "not every pain comes to harm you," which I guess was his favorite Sicilian phrase. I'd heard it enough over the years.

The date had lasted way longer than I'd expected. Not a bad thing, not at all. Brian seemed like a pretty good guy, and because of that, I'd taken a risk and said out loud half of everything that came to mind during our dinner. That I was the one who suggested dinner and spoke the words that we should see each other again, well... who am I? Was I becoming bold? Brave? Desperate?

Ten months of disappointment had brought me full circle in my beliefs about a lifelong love. Maybe that wasn't in the cards for me. Gosh, my negativity was trying to kill the awesome Brian mood. The gin and wine were messing with my head, which spun like the earth was inside me.

I desperately needed to talk about everything with Sylvie. We've been there for each other through thick and thin. Occasionally, I even remind her that if it hadn't been my phone call to Pete, she might still be searching for Mr. Right. But what did I really know about relationships and love? "Niente" is what my ancestors would say. Nothing.

My car's clock glowed white, telling me that nine o'clock was fast approaching. Sylvie, the early riser, liked to be in bed by ten her time while I preferred to welcome each new day as the shiny digits on my clock switched to twelve-oh-one. At the last red light before home, I beat the radio's rhythm on my steering wheel. Knowing I'd get to talk to her that night, my breathing slowed, anxiety ticking down a few notches. I had no idea what I was doing and a dating emergency or two or three loomed ahead. What if I'd already totally screwed up things with Jake and Brian?

"Sylvie, please, please answer when I call," I whispered as I turned into our driveway, tires squealing on wet cement. I hurried to the house through a curtain of steady rain, not bothering with the unwieldy task of opening an umbrella.

I pushed the front door closed, clicked the deadbolt, and listened to the sounds coming from down the hall. My parents were talking at the kitchen table when I poked my head in to say good night. Mom stood as she offered to fix me a glass of water, but I waved her off and faked a yawn.

"Off to bed." I didn't want to confess how much I needed to talk to Sylvie right then.

I slipped damp feet out of wet ballerina-style shoes and dialed her number. Tossing the phone onto my pink comforter, I started undressing. I'd wash my face later.

My call went to voicemail. What the…? A knot twisted in my stomach. Could I even get to sleep without the balm of Sylvie's advice? I didn't believe so.

The bathroom door stood open across from my bedroom. When I was a kid, I practiced tossing clothes and toys between rooms. The hot water always took a minute to make it to my faucet, so I used the time to remove my contact lenses. Smearing cleanser on my cheeks, I bent to add warm water and executed my nightly makeup removal routine.

While drying my hands, my phone rang. The blues tune I'd selected long ago offered me a trill of piano keys that always made me smile. That night, my phone's music made me grin bigger than a kid at Christmas. Sylvie was returning my call.

"So-rr-y, I was in the tub."

"Sylvie, thank goodness. I thought I was in for a sleepless night!"

"Whoa. What's the matter?"

Pulling back the bedcovers, I climbed onto my bed and leaned against the upholstered headboard I'd crafted last year during a mercifully brief do-it-yourself phase. Furniture had gotten way too expensive and my six-figure moving out savings goal remained elusive. I'd watched an adorable rancher come on and off the market for the last ten years, and the sales price kept climbing.

"I've got two guys!"

"Two? That's good, right?"

"I don't know what to do, and I agreed to go hiking on Sunday. I'm going to make a total fool of myself. His best friend was a girl. How messed up is that?"

"Whoa again. Calm down, Ang. Deep breath."

I inhaled noisily through my nose and out of my mouth, pressing my back hard against the pillows behind me.

"Now, start at the beginning. Who are the two guys?"

"Okay. Hang on a minute." I stood beside my bed and reached toward the ceiling, then tilted my head in every direction: front, back, right, left. "Thanks. I'm back."

"Stretching?"

"Uh-huh," I said with a small smile. A therapist had taught me the technique when, as a middle schooler, I dealt with incessant, almost paralyzing anxiety. The simplicity and familiarity of the movements had yet to fail in settling my nerves.

"So-o-o...?"

"First date was a guy named Jake. He manages a restaurant and has blond dreadlocks. Very cute. Bright blue eyes and a tan! He kinda looked like a skier or surfer. Very funny. I laughed a lot.”

“Wow, he sounds great. You liked him. Are you going on the hike with him?”

“Nope. That’s Brian. We had dinner tonight. Oh, Sylvie, I was bold. Well, bold for me.”

“Really?”

Shivering, I pulled the comforter up around me. I let out my breath.

“We sat at the bar for a drink. That was all we were there for. I liked him. He was easy to be with, so I asked if he wanted to stay there for dinner. He didn’t hesitate, took control, got our name on the list and in no time, we were seated at a perfect corner table by a window.”

“Pretty awesome, huh?”

“Yeah,” I whispered, flames of fear scorching the edges of my thoughts. I wasn’t sure how to handle one guy, and there I was, considering dating two nice guys. I needed Sylvie’s help to figure things out.

“What’re you thinking right now?”

“How do I, Angie Caruso, date two guys at the same time? I mean, Sylvie, can I string along...”

“Hey, hey. I think you’re getting ahead of yourself here. Slow down.”

I took a deep breath, put the phone on my bed, and clasped my hands above my head.

“Ooh-kay, calming breath. I’m good. I think.”

Sylvie giggled.

“I’ll figure this out. I will, won’t I, Sylvie?”

“Yes, you will figure this out. It’s not rocket science, but it is definitely hard. Let’s not pretend that figuring out dating or love is anything but difficult.”

“Stop. Right. There. I’m dying here. Should I book dates with them both? Should I go hiking? Hiking, Sylvie. Me outdoors. I can’t even. And please, no love talk.”

“Ang. Tell me about this guy... um, Brian?”

I told her about his shiny black hair and icy blue eyes. He was average height, not too tall. Not skinny, kinda solidly built. He seemed physically strong, but perhaps that's just the idea of him being outdoors a lot.

"He sounds amazing," Sylvie said as she yawned.

"Oh lord, I'm keeping you up. It's way past your bed-time."

"No, I'm here for you. You and Brian exchanged num-bers, so will he contact you before Sunday? Did he say anything about it, or did you catch a vibe?"

"Maybe?" I stood again to stretch. "I dunno," I whined to my best friend. How am I supposed to know anything about what a guy's gonna do?

"Okay, consider this. It doesn't matter if he does or not. Just prepare for Sunday, that's all."

"Prepare? I don't have time to shop."

"No shopping required. You have walking shoes, right?"

"Boy, this sure sounds familiar, but the tables are turned." I'd helped Sylvie shop last year for a date outfit. Over the phone, that is.

"They are! I'd almost forgotten. But listen, just go through your clothes and find a pair of sweatpants or track pants, you know. Or jeans. I think it's all about layers on a fall hike."

"Wow, you've looked at hiking apparel?"

"Not really, but Pete took me to the mountains on Valentine's Day. Remember? I looked online for outfit ideas. And I was totally fine."

I grinned, thinking about what Pete did on the big day, but I didn't say anything. I have a tendency to push her buttons and then she pushes back.

I laughed as I plopped back onto my bed. My anxiety had finally tamped down. Thanks to Sylvie. And then my phone dinged. The message from Jake made me groan Sylvie's name.

"Sylvie...it's starting."

"What's starting?"

"Double man trouble," I whined for the second time that night. "A text from Jake."

"What did he say?"

"Hello."

Sylvie laughed, then apologized.

"Right. So not funny."

"How about it's 'fun' instead? Switch up your attitude and embrace new adventures ahead."

"Ugh to adventure." I walked over to my turntable and put on a jazz record, sliding the volume down so as not to disturb my parents. They'd passed by a little earlier, and Mom had scratched my door with her nails as a "good night."

"You don't mean that, Ang. You wouldn't be on Flirtable at all if you weren't open to new things. And a hike sure is an adventure for you, which you agreed to. You're growing. Wow, think how we've both grown in the past year!"

"Okay, okay. What do I say?"

"Just say 'hi' back. And if he keeps texting, I can let you go."

"I may need you to coach me."

"No, you absolutely do not need me for that. Did you text back?"

"Hang on... okay," I said, letting out a loud breath. The whoosh filled my room as my message crossed to the other side of Birmingham.

Staring at my phone, I forgot all about Sylvie on the other line.

"Earth to Angie," Sylvie called to me.

"Oh, I'm so sorry. My anxiety is ready to go through the roof. Again."

"You'll be fine," Sylvie's soothing voice was interrupted by another ding on my phone.

"He asked if I'm up for a drink on next Thursday night. Phew. I was so afraid he'd ask me out on Sunday!" I pulled a pillow over my head. "I can't take this."

"You're worrying about things that have not happened, my friend. And probably won't either."

"I know. I'm being stupid."

"Not stupid, just out of practice. You'll do just fine. Hey, have fun with this."

"Thanks, Sylvie. I wrote him back and agreed on a time and place. He sent a thumbs up emoji."

"So romantic. L-O-L!"

"Stop," I moaned.

"Gonna let you go now, Angie. I need my beauty sleep."

"Good night. I'll call you after the hike."

"Can't wait!"

After we hung up, I shut down the music. I did my final before-bed stretch and slipped under the covers. Pondering the idea of cool air on my face on Sunday, I shivered. I'd survive it; how hard could it be?

My vision of cool air on cheeks came true more than even my wild and anxious imagination had conjured. I met Brian in a wide-open parking lot off the highway on Sunday morning at nine-thirty. No buildings or slopes blocked the chilly wind from flipping the ends of my black plaid scarf around my face.

"Hey," Brian greeted me as he stood beside the passenger door of his dark green pickup. Offering me a hand, he helped me up into a tan leather bucket seat. I tucked my gloved hands between my legs.

"You're committed, I'll say that," I quipped as he slid into the driver's seat.

Hands on the steering wheel, he turned and smiled. "Glad you made it. I kinda wondered if you'd cancel."

"What? Me?"

Brian laughed heartily and turned the ignition key. The big truck's engine purred to life.

"The temp's really dipped today. It's a cold front or something. You sure you'll be okay? Looks like you dressed the part."

"Thanks. I'll be fine. Well, I hope so."

"I got you." He looked me straight in the eye, and I held his gaze until I couldn't anymore. I looked down and laced my fingers together.

"Where are you taking me?"

"Ever been to Ruffner Mountain?"

"Uh, no. But I have heard of it. It's not far, I know that."

"Right, we'll be there in fifteen." Brian pulled the truck out of the lot and headed us back to the highway. I noted that we drove north, so I'd remember to tell Sylvie. I'm so directionally challenged, I'd never figure out how to navigate back to wherever we were going or find my way back to the car later.

The truck was silent but for the whirring of the tires on pavement. Brian didn't have the radio on, so I ventured into interview mode.

"What kind of music do you usually listen to?"

He reached immediately for the radio button on the dashboard. "You want music on?"

"Oh no, that's not what I meant. Just asking what you like."

"Here, let me turn it on and you can click all my presets." He offered me a curious look.

I flipped around his radio stations, finding an eclectic set of options. With my eye on the radio, I could stay quiet and take calming breaths. Being alone with Brian in his truck cab sent me into sensory overload. He smelled good and

I couldn't put a name to it. Me clueless, who spent days around hundreds of candles at the store.

"Hm. Interesting."

"Interesting good or interesting bad?"

We chuckled in unison.

"Just teasin'. I listen to at least half of those myself." I gave him a thumbs up.

"Did I just pass a test?"

"Music is important. My parents introduced to me to all kinds when I was growing up. I watched them dance around the kitchen a lot. Very heartwarming."

"Sounds like it. My parents didn't do a lot of dancing 'round our house, but they have such a solid relationship. They probably ruined me for my own future relationships."

"You believe that? Your ideals might be too high?"

Brian shrugged. The clicking of the blinker filled the cab.

"Oh, we're already here." My tummy tightened when I looked across the parking lot. Near a wooden sign, a small group had gathered. One girl left them and started toward Brian's truck, straight blonde hair blowing around her face. Her smile faltered when I opened my door and hopped to the ground.

"Brian!" Blonde girl exclaimed. She trotted up to his door as he climbed out.

"Hey, Kayla." I could barely hear him, but he sounded neutral, a good sign. As I came around the front bumper, Kayla dropped her hand from his forearm. She'd said something private to him, I thought. Brian looked up from adjusting his gloves, a strange look on his face. Well, it probably wasn't strange, but out-of-practice-me had no idea how to interpret it.

"Angie, this is Kayla. She's a founder of this group."

"Hi, Kayla. This is my first hike!" I thrust out my hand in greeting and she stared for a beat before taking it. Certain I'd seen a flicker of delight on her face because I'd admitted my hiking ignorance, I slid my arm into the crook of Brian's and fixed that. Oh yeah, sassy Angie is here.

"I'm sure Brian'll take good care of me," I cooed and hated myself a little for acting like a girly-girl. Sylvie and I had rolled eyes at the girls who swooned over boys in high school. And here I was, someone who knew better, doing the same thing more than a decade later.

"Yeah. Let's go meet the others and get started." Brian didn't pull away, so we walked up to the other nine hikers arm in arm, all the while a butterfly skipped its wings against my insides, the tickling feeling more pleasurable than I could've imagined. This is only our second date, and these feelings made me wonder if I should stumble into panic mode.

The day's hike leader, Mike, had us all introduce ourselves. He briefly described the path and conditions and asked if all were ready. I enthusiastically nodded.

"We'll sweep," Brian said. The group turned to the trailhead, and Brian held back.

"What does sweep mean?"

Brian looked at me with the kindest expression. "Don't worry. It just means we'll be bringing up the rear, ensuring no one straggles too far back."

"Oh."

"What did you think it meant?" Amusement lightened his question.

"Clean up on aisle six!" I hung my head, laughing at myself.

Brian flung his arm around my shoulders, grinning. "We'll make you a hiker."

I didn't know yet if I wanted to be a hiker, but I definitely enjoyed being with Brian. We walked and talked along the shady path, the weak October sun shimmering between half-bare branches.

"Brian!" Kayla's voice penetrated our bubble.

"Yeah!" He yelled back loud enough that I decided to pull away, pretending to look at the plants on the trail's edge.

Kayla paused for us to catch up and positioned herself between Brian and me as we continued behind the others. Lots of laughter and chatter preceded us on the leaf-covered path, but fear of tripping forced my head down, watching where I was walking on the rocky dirt trail. Kayla gossiped about one of the couples ahead of us. I paid little attention to her until I heard her mention Mount Cheaha. I'd been to the state park there with a middle school science class, but we hadn't climbed very far up Alabama's highest mountain.

Instead of butting in, I hung back. I could ask Brian about it on the ride back to my car. So far, this little hiking outing wasn't so bad. Well, except for Kayla, who was stealing my date with her tight black pants, cute hiking boots, and puffy red jacket — catalog model style right there on the trail. How old was she? Twenty-something? I shook my head as I slowed down and became the "sweep" for this hike.

Brian touched Kayla's shoulder and hitched his head back toward me. "Talk to you later. Lemme get back to Angie."

Keeping my expression neutral proved difficult when my heart pounded excitedly inside my chest. He was with me, and I liked the idea of it. I appreciated Brian's warmth and fun-loving attitude, though I did wonder about the girl best friend from college. Not sure I'd get past that anytime soon. Perhaps one day I'd have the nerve to explore it with him. He seemed willing to talk about anything so far.

Chapter 5

Brian

A WARMER-THAN-AVERAGE OCTOBER MORNING was just what this guy had ordered. Angie had acted a little less than enthused about the hike when I first invited her. I understood her doubt about going out with a group of strangers on a chilly Sunday, doing an activity she'd never done.

Hikers are a friendly sort, so bringing a guest unannounced didn't matter to the group. Kayla acted weird though — too chatty and clingy — cutting into my time with Angie. Why she didn't get that I had brought a date to the hike puzzled me. I considered Kayla's behavior after I dropped Angie at her car and headed back to my condo.

She's ten years younger, and I'd never given her much attention, even though I seemed to be her favorite hiking buddy. Sometimes she prevented me from talking to other hikers, but I haven't made an issue of it. Maybe I'd encouraged her too much by giving in to her being my hiking partner.

I suspect plenty of other guys on our hikes would love to chat her up, but she'd hitched herself to my wagon, and I'd done nothing about it. Some might say I let it happen and played along to get some ego boost from the attention of a young woman—a beautiful one, at that.

But Angie was as lovely as Kayla. I've dated plenty of blondes, but the gravitational pull of dark hair and warm eyes was indisputable. Angie had all that in spades—dark wavy hair brushing her slim neck and big brown eyes that reminded me of those in the dolls my cousins had played with. I'm five-eleven, and I'd guess Angie was barely five-two, which was also attractive in that she brought out the protective side of me.

My phone rang when I was about fifteen minutes from home, so I hit the answer button on the dash and said, "Hey, Mike. Good trail, man."

"Looked like you were having one. Two chicks hanging on you. Who was the newbie?"

"Angie, we met online. That, my friend, was a date. Our second."

"Really? So...what about Kayla?"

"Kayla what? We've never..."

Mike snorted a laugh.

"Seriously, man, I have not encouraged Kayla. Never asked her out and always ignored her private messages to me on the hiking site. Nothin' going on there."

"Well, the other guys'll be happy to hear it. Kayla sure gave a different impression. Wishful thinkin' on her part. Is that what you're saying?"

I beat my hand on the steering wheel. "Idiot," I whispered.

"Right. Didn't know she was wishing anything."

"Man, you are one clueless dude." He chuckled again, and while it was tempting to fume at Mike, I chuckled along with him.

"Call me stupid, I guess."

"Stupid. Haha."

I rubbed a hand over my face. The traffic light ahead changed to red, and I grunted as I slammed on the brakes.

"You okay?" Mike asked.

"Yeah. Red light. Kinda like life, ya know. Warning, warning. Women, danger." I laughed. I was so out of my depth, and I didn't know how to traverse those deep waters. Oh, I'd always believed I understood women on a deeper level, but I'd been blind of late. I hoped I hadn't hurt Kayla's feelings.

"You got that right. Hey, I gotta go. I'm meeting my wife at the grocery store. Weekly shopping duty."

"What's your wife's name? I've never asked. Sorry, man."

"Mary. She's a saint."

"To put up with you—"

"For sure. See ya next weekend?"

"Yep. Be there."

That right there, that conversation, was a revelation. I didn't remember that Mike was married. Some friend I was. We'd had beers together after a few hikes. I strained to remember what we'd talked about.

My brothers remained in Tuscaloosa, where my parents lived in the same house we grew up in. John, the eldest at forty, was married with two young kids: Sam, ten, and Jillian, eight. The middle brother, Nick, got married last December. What a fun wedding that was!

Anyway, those two were still my best friends. Since I started working in the engineering department at the hydroelectric plant in Vincent five years ago, I've made a few new friends that I can hang with. They're all married, every last one of them. Some days at work, the guys make me feel like the lone survivor — I'm the only one who's got freedom, apparently.

Well, sure. I'm free to sit at home every night and click the remote to another game or law drama. Interviewing potential dates on Flirtable was fun at first until it wasn't anymore. I didn't realize scanning women's profiles was going to be so much work, but then again, the last thing I wanted to do was surf the glossy wooden bars of downtown Birmingham looking for love. Too much like college frat parties where dozens of scantily clad coeds showed up with big hair and war paint. I know. I sound like a misogynist, but to be honest, I wanted what was best for those young women. Somehow, I got the over-protective gene. So, no, I would never be caught trolling for women at bars.

But that's what all my work buddies think I'm doing. Living it up as a bar-hopping single guy. My life is not that interesting, besides all the outdoors action I get. Action as in exercise and fresh air with like-minded people. Yet, so far, in the years I've lived and played around Birmingham, no like-minded woman has stolen her way into my heart. And I was ready for that to happen.

I never — absolutely never — say anything to these guys about how jealous I am of their lives. Every June, my employer hosts a family cookout and games day. I have taken a date only once in the five summers I've attended that event, and I won't do that again until I find the right woman. The employee summer parties have been a lot of fun, and I got my biggest kicks out of playing with the kids of my friends. They seem to think I'm all right too, as evidenced by what happened at last year's party.

Josiah, the son of a fellow engineer, ran up to me with a small foam football, yelling, "Brian! Brian! Can you practice passing with me?"

"Hey, bud. Where's your dad and mom?"

He brushed sweaty blond hair out of his eyes and squinted as he gazed across the long grass yard that led down to a river bank. "I dunno. C'mon, play with me. You're the best. Please?" Josiah stuck out his bottom lip, like he knew exactly what he was doing.

How could I say no to the kid? Since I didn't have a date to tend to, I tossed around the football with Josiah for fifteen minutes, then whispered into his ear that dear ol' uncle Brian needed a beer, which made the eight-year-old cackle like his dad. I tousled his blond curls and held up my hand for a high-five.

"Later, dude," Josiah said in a grownup voice. I could've kidnapped that kid for his cuteness.

Kids, it would appear, like me. Take my nephew and niece, they hijack my brother's phone calls all the time to tell me their own news. One might believe they have more exciting lives than I do, and of course I show interest and offer wild praise for all their antics and achievements.

Let's just say it's mutual admiration with most kids I know. I'm just a kid at heart. I put that in my profile on Flirtable. Perhaps it kept some women out of the running, but, hey, that's okay. If you don't want to live a little and let your hair down sometimes, then we are not meant to be.

As I jogged up the stairs to my third-floor con-do—avoiding the elevator everywhere was sport to me—I groaned about my philosophical mood. I should be cele-brating that second date with a pretty woman. Once inside my apartment, I removed my layers and head for the show-er, wondering what my lunch might be. I could still smell the bacon I'd reheated and nibbled on before the hike.

I smiled when an image of "Hiking Angie" entered my mind again. I suspected she struggled a little on the hike. But she acted like she had a good time even though she huffed and puffed on some of the steepest inclines on the trail. I could tell she was tired as heck when it was all over.

While I drove her back to her car, I claimed credit for the glorious weather. She'd smirked and said, "Oh yeah, just like summer." To which I'd replied, "Just wait. Summer hikes can be outstanding, plus we plan for lots of shade and many cool-down water breaks. It's beastly when the temp's over 90, I'll grant you that. I'm still out there, though!" She didn't seem impressed.

Angie let me walk her to her car in the lot, placing the driver's side door between us. I noticed things like that.

Her protective move didn't bother me, not exactly. I wish that I could have given her a quick hug or kiss on the cheek. Women should set the rules early in relationships, and when I respect that, I've learned I can get another date.

That said, Angie didn't commit to hiking with the group the next Sunday, claiming she had to check her calendar. I'd have to be patient.

I grinned as I remembered her body against mine as she responded to Kayla when they met. She'd looped her arm through mine and got a little sassy. What did she say? I searched my memory. Oh, brother. I am a stupid idiot. Angie had detected Kayla's romantic dreams in a few seconds and I'd missed it for months. Women and their superior radar—that's what my brother John always says, and I hadn't understood what he meant until after that hike.

No wonder I'm single, I chastised myself while I showered. I breathed the hot steam in to open my head.

Two o'clock was a little late to eat lunch, especially since I planned to stuff myself with junk at my brother John's house that night. Our favorite college football rivalry had arrived. I lived an hour away from John, and the drive was all freeway — easy. But suddenly it didn't seem easy or pleasant. I grabbed my cell phone off the granite counter and sent off a text message.

Hi Angie, thanks for hiking with me today!

Silence. I left my phone on the counter and opened the sliding door onto my deck. Soft sunshine greeted me, so I stepped onto the concrete in sock feet. Wrapping my hands around the railing, I tensed my arms and did a few standing pushups. The atmosphere was heavy with the loamy scent of falling leaves, reminding me of the fresh air between me and Angie while we pressed forward up an uneven, root-laden path.

I watched a neighbor park his car and unload plastic bags from his back seat. He held up a hand in greeting when he spotted me peering down at him. Everyone's grocery shopping, I thought. Knowing I had a busy Sunday, I'd hit up the store early the day before.

Half an hour later, my phone pinged, and I couldn't get to it fast enough.

Thanks for inviting me. I enjoyed it. And brr...

She ended the text with a blue freezing emoji. It hadn't been that chilly, had it? I took a deep breath and plowed forward with my question.

So, it's a big game day for Alabama and I'm going to my brother's. Would you like to come with me? It's an hour each way. It's a lot to ask.

Sure she'd turn me down, I tried to make it easy for her to do so. I thought so, anyway.

The three dots bounced on the screen, then disappeared. I put the phone down, so I wouldn't start sweating the stupid stuff. It dinged.

I appreciate the invite. But I'm beat, and I have stuff to do before I start the work week.

My loud, disappointed sigh startled me. I'd been holding my breath. I reread her message, wondering if she'd hidden any affection in her words.

It was a long shot, but I had to ask. You have a great evening.

Thanks, Brian. Drive safe!

Hey, don't forget to check your calendar for next weekend.

I rubbed my eyes, hoping she'd just say yes. I kept pushing her, and I had no idea when I'd hit Angie's no-way wall.

I will. It's at work, so....

Dang. I sent her a thumbs-up emoji and got ready to leave.

Apparently, dating required some patience, and just how little of that did I possess?

Chapter 6

Angie

I DROVE HOME WITH the windows down, enjoying the Alabama weather. At the start of the hike, the temperature had been almost too cold, but when we hit the occasional pocket of sunshine, it wasn't so bad. After an hour, it hit the fifty degrees the forecaster had promised. I'd worked up a sweat because those people — those crazy hikers could walk fast. Brian had mentioned the pace was brisk, but the actual pace fit in the what-the-heck category. I hadn't known what I was getting into, obviously.

What's that saying about a walk in the woods? Who said that? Emerson, perhaps. Stupid questions enter my head and then I have to explore them later. Jeepers.

Sylvie's gonna want to hear the whole story. Since we've been friends for so long, I hardly have to think about it. The words would spill out and she'd be forced to ask questions about what I meant. All my feelings flowing across the phone line made her crazy.

And I did have a lot of feelings about my hiking date. Brian was kind and patient with me. My ignorance probably amused him, but he answered my questions and acted like he enjoyed explaining all things hiking. My other feelings were about that bimbo, Kayla. What was with her? I hoped Sylvie had some insight, particularly how to handle her on the next hike.

Next hike? Was I already considering that torture in a positive light? Brian earned all positive marks from me. Except the Kayla thing. He seemed a little oblivious to her crush. I mean, it was so obvious, a person would have to be deaf and blind not to pick up on her interest.

Everyone in the group was friendly and obviously cared about each other. They knew interesting tidbits about each other's lives. At least that's what my eavesdropping gathered over the course of two hours. Because of Kayla, I ended up on my own. Then I found myself beside another friendly hiker who didn't hesitate to ask me personal questions, like how I met Brian.

Unsure of what Brian shared about his dating life, I wasn't about to disclose that we met online. I lied and said, "mutual friends," considering it was partially true since my dear Sylvie was the one who convinced me to try the dating site. Okay, it was a bald-faced lie. Down the road, perhaps I would ask Brian what he thought about revealing the truth of how we met. Assuming there is a "down the road" where that conversation might take place.

Once I got to my bedroom, my fingers hit the call button on my phone.

"Sylvie!"

"Angie, I've been in agony waiting."

"I literally just got home from the hike. Agony, really? Isn't Pete there to keep you distracted from silly Angie worry?"

"You coulda called me from the car." Sylvie's chastisement was laced with a teasing tone.

"Yeah, yeah. And where's Pete?"

"He had to go to New York. Again."

"More movie stuff?"

"I guess. And she's going to be in the meetings."

"Evelyn? Well, she's his ex and you're his fiancé. The end."

Sylvie sighed. "You're right."

"Don't be jealous of her. Trust Pete. He's one of the good ones."

"True enough. I'm acting stupid. How was the date?"

"Besides hard work? It was okay." I kicked off my sneakers and found the tread stuffed with rocks and dirt. Oh brother, the hike still lingered in my life. I rolled my eyes.

"Merely okay?"

"I'm sorry. Still recovering. And there was this girl."

"Uh-oh."

"Exactly. Kayla. Tall, skinny, blonde. Crushing on Brian, so it appeared to me."

"What'd she do? Butt-in on your date?"

"Kinda, kinda not. On the hike, everyone talked to everyone, so keeping him all to myself wasn't gonna happen. Though Kayla got in between us at one point, and I lagged back, observing all the dimensions of a group hike."

"What? You did not, Angela Caruso. Why would you hang back?"

"It hurt my feelings at first that Brian let her stay, and he didn't get rid of her fast."

"Of course! What's wrong with him, too?"

"Too? Okay, I'll take the criticism. But you weren't there, Sylvie. He knew everyone. My expectations were... well, it wasn't as bad as I imagined, besides being slightly freezing early on. The fresh air did me some actual good. I stay cooped up way too much."

"I get it. How were you to behave, especially on a second date? Don't beat yourself up."

"I'm not going to. When he realized I wasn't right there, he told Kayla to buzz off and hung back with me."

"He told her that?"

"Not exactly, but she left us alone afterwards. I had to share him with a couple of other people briefly. If anyone believed we were on a date, they had telepathy. We didn't look like we were on a date."

"In a bad way or—"

"Being in a big group of hikers made us look like nothing, I suppose. I could've been his sister."

"Okay, so it was kinda weird. But not bad, right? Goin' out again?"

"He asked me on another hike next Sunday. And I agreed to have a drink with Jake on Thursday. I may cancel that. I dunno how my life will turn out and that stresses me."

"Deep breath, my friend."

I breathed deeply through my nose and out of my mouth.

"That's my girl."

"I think I'll say yes to the hike, but it can't be hiking all the time. It was really hard to learn anything about him."

"Did you watch him? You usually have great radar about people."

"Years of customers, girl. I picked up on a few things. Everybody likes him, loves him even. The ones I chatted with sang his praises. Could he be too perfect? That would not be good either. Would it?"

"Now, now, don't get carried away. What's wrong with a little perfection? Like my Pete!" Sylvie laughed.

Sylvie was right. I was over-analyzing again instead of going with the flow. Staying buried in inventory and accounting numbers every week had trained me to look for problems to fix. Or run away from, as had been the case with most of my dating history.

"You're right. I'm going to give Brian and Jake a chance, in case one of them is Mr. Right. Your brand of success could also be mine."

"Wow, way to turn it around, Ang."

"Check with me in an hour and see if I'm still there mentally," I said as I flopped down on my bed. I'd sorted my laundry and paced in front of my window until I was tired of the view. I looked down at the sage green carpet, sure that I could see a flat spot where I'd been pacing.

"What does your heart say?"

"My heart? I really like him, Sylvie. Really, really like him. He's...he's so warm and I kind of... um, feel safe. Safe? Is that the right way to feel about a guy you recently met? Is that even romantic?"

"Hmm. It's interesting. Go with it and see how that sense grows or disappears over your next few dates."

"Such a good friend."

"Trying to help you like you helped me last year."

"Oh Sylvie, so sorry I didn't let you finish your story about you and Pete. I'm all ears."

"Nothing else to tell. We had dinner the night before he left for New York, um, Wednesday. I went to church with his mom this morning. I do love her."

"Brunch too?"

"Not today."

"What color nails are we going to wear for your wedding?" I asked, changing the subject.

"Maybe deep red? You know, to match the dresses."

I shrugged. I understood her traditional view of it, but I was hoping for a natural nail. It's her wedding. Perhaps I could sell the idea when she came down for the bridal shower. Yikes, I needed to finish up some things for that since it was only two weeks away.

"I'll think about the red. Wonder what your sister wants? Listen, I should get my laundry done and think about what I'm wearing on Thursday. Planning ahead wards off worry."

"See ya, kiddo."

Sylvie and I ended our call and most likely we both strode to our washing machines to begin the Sunday laundry chore. I stopped in the kitchen for a piece of fried chicken out of the fridge. Mom and Dad were out on their usual Sunday brunch date with friends. Mom was so lucky to be free of work, and Dad would be retired sooner rather than later. I rested both elbows on the oak kitchen table and sighed loudly. I'd get my turn. One day. In thirty years.

My phone buzzed, so I wiped my greasy fingers on a napkin before flipping it over. It was Brian. Football game? Good heavens... with his family? I rested my forehead on my hands, exasperated. With me or him, both of us? Clearly, we liked each other, or we may have craved more time together. But I needed to put on the brakes of this blooming relationship. The speed Brian moved was making my heart pitter-patter way too fast and hard. There was a bit of insta-love going on with him, and it scared me. What if it burned out as fast as it started? I begged off, pleading work stuff.

The afternoon actually loomed ahead without any plans. I figured I'd watch some of the football game with my parents. I thought about taking a nap, so I didn't have to agonize over two men. Then I remembered I hadn't even checked my profile on Flirtable in three days. Instead of dealing with the chance of more troubling questions, I slipped under a blanket on the sofa and dozed off.

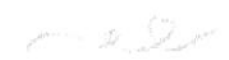

The first of the week flew by in a blur of customers, nothing to complain about for sure. What possesses people to wait until they have only a day or two to buy holiday home decor? We've had fall decor out since August — okay, I admit we retailers are the true ruination of every holiday with our early merchandizing. Dad was out with a cold, and our part-time stock helper had left town to visit his sick mother. Deliveries of Christmas merchandise overflowed the stockrooms, and I failed miserably to help Dad keep that organized. I was busier than a one-armed wallpaper hanger.

As I was so distracted the day before Halloween, my mobile phone disappeared under piles of paperwork on my desk. My attention was required on the floor, and I never noticed I was flying phone-less. That probably has a name with the kids nowadays, but I was unaware that my messaging app was on fire with texts from Sylvie. Then the store phone rang, and Vanessa took the call.

I heard Vanessa on the phone and thought nothing of it until she appeared at my side, holding the wireless handset in her hand, apologizing.

"I'm sorry to interrupt, ma'am. Angie, you need to go to your office."

My eyebrows creased together in a frown since she'd stepped into my conversation with a long-time customer. Mrs. Ragland was also close friends with my mom.

"Seriously, Angie, go to your office and check your cell phone. It's Sylvie's mother. An emergency."

"Oh my goodness, Mrs. Ragland, I'm so sorry. Do you mind if Vanessa finishes helping you with your project? She'll take good care of you, I promise." I nodded toward my assistant and walked backwards for a few seconds until they fell into conversation. I scooted quickly to my office. Vanessa's cheerful voice and the laughter of Mrs. Ragland made me feel better about deserting a faithful customer.

My office looked like a bomb had gone off, releasing reams of paper of various shades of white and yellow. My phone dinged, and I swiped through pages and pages of, let's call it what it was... an abominable mess. I needed more help, which I'd been too scared to ask for, given Dad's emphatic "no" a year ago.

My phone fell onto the padded mat under my rolling chair, and I snatched it up. My messages app showed a red circle and the number five. I frowned, wondering whatever had happened in the outside world while I sold fall garlands and pumpkins, and... so much stuff.

I had messages from both Sylvie's mother and sister. Sigh.

After I scrolled through the messages, which included two extremely long texts from Mrs. Bradley relaying her conversation with the florist. Apparently, they'd run into each other at the grocery store.

With the way I'd been doubting my ability to do pretty much anything effectively, I was relieved to know she hadn't been checking up behind my back. It'd be just like her to do it, though. Tears tickled my lashes. Tossing my phone onto my desk, I walked to the window and watched the foot traffic strolling by. The door chimed in the background and Vanessa's greeting made me smile at having such a reliable coworker.

I pondered how to respond to Mrs. B and Constance Miller. I hit the call button for Sylvie's sister, hoping for a little less drama. While the phone rang at the other end, I dug around for the red file folder holding all my notes and receipts for the bridal shower. I found it as Constance Miller picked up.

The call was brief, ending with her promise to call her momma and let her know I'd handle things. Then I had to keep my promise. My careful review of the contract quickly revealed the problem. A stray mark turned the centerpiece quantity of six to sixteen. I should have caught that.

I grabbed my coat and called out to Vanessa. She peeked her head from behind a table display.

"Yeah?"

"I'm headed down the street to Flora. Gotta fix a bridal shower problem."

"Oh no. That's why Mrs. Bradley called?"

"Uh, huh."

"Good luck!"

"Thanks," I said as I pulled open the door. The blasted, overly-cheerful chime drowned out my appreciation.

Blowing out a breath, I stopped on the sidewalk and looked both ways. The street possessed the deepest sense of home for me. I'd played under the awning of the barber shop across the street decades ago. Faded now, the red and blue scallops fluttered in a comfortable October breeze. I wished that the street boasted trees along the sidewalk, but the city had nixed that idea of Mom's back when I was a toddler. The park a block away became the green-space solution ten years after she made her original request. Let's pause for a moment of silence in appreciation of the glacial-speed of government.

I zipped past that park and made a left off the main shopping street. Flora, the flower shop my family always used, occupied a tiny space on a corner. I've always loved the angled corner door, almost exotic to my younger self — certainly rare in the four-block radius I was finally allowed to traverse alone upon turning fifteen. The most special part of that doorway, however, was how it transported me into paradise—heavenly scents that assailed seemingly every pore of my body. Surely I'd get a chance to stick my head into one of the chillers to smell the roses.

"Uh-oh" chimed as I opened the door, making me smile. Florence, the owner, had a sense of humor with that choice of doorbell. Our electronic chime didn't offer the "uh-oh" version, to my chagrin. Not that Dad would allow it. I wish he—

"Angela, doll-baby." Florence, known to me as Miss Flo, came around from behind the counter, her full body encased in a fuchsia smock over wide-legged denims. She certainly had a style. I smiled anxiously. The knot in my stomach leaped into my throat. With only two weeks to go, I worried flowers had been ordered that I'd be on the hook for, and honestly, I couldn't afford it. Especially if I had to dip into my savings. I've always been proud of my thrifty habits. I had moving plans for that growing nest egg—fresh flowers were not part of the plan.

"Hi Miss Flo," I said meekly, giving her a little wave.

"Come on in here and talk to me." Florence patted on a stool by the counter, its painted paisley pattern a riot of rainbow hues.

I pulled out the contract as I slid my bottom onto the hard seat. "So I—"

She held up a hand. "It's fixed."

"It is? I just heard today about the sixteen centerpieces mistake. I'm so sorry if you already ordered materials. All that Christmas stuff filling your store in November."

"I had, that's true."

"Well, um—"

"Hon, it's fixed," she interrupted again.

"But how? I don't want you to lose money."

She chuckled and shook her head. "Miss Flo ain't never gonna lose some money, child. I just won't order the greenery for another customer and use yours. Customers care more about the flowers than the greenery, anyway. It'll be fine. As for the flowers, I signed up for the altar arrangement down at my Second Baptist, so I'll just switch up the flowers I'd planned for that."

"But still, that's a lot of flowers."

"You kept it simple, so there will be other customers to buy. Red flowers are always in style. Don't you worry that little head about it. We good."

I inhaled a shaky breath, filling my head with the store's aromas—loam and the sugar-sweet scent of lilies on the counter. I shook my head. "I'm so sorry for missing that detail. I've been overwhelmed," I confessed.

"Time for tea?"

"Tea?"

"Pot's brewing in back." She looked at the clock over the storeroom door, its white face and simple black hands announcing three o'clock. The afternoon was racing by and I had so much to do.

"Sure." I slid off the stool to follow her. "So long as the sniffs are free."

The flower queen I'd loved for years cackled as she pushed the saloon-style doors into the back area.

Like Mom, Miss Flo knew the power of tea to wash away stress... and the occasional tears.

Chapter 7

Brian

Special days come and go all the time, but Halloween isn't special like Valentine's Day, definitely the day you need someone to share it with. Why couldn't Halloween be that kind of holiday, too?

I rode by Angie's store, lights still ablaze at six in the evening and customers exiting onto the sidewalk with red and white bags sporting the store logo, a swirl of the letters M, M, and C. I didn't see Angie, of course, and I was tempted to stop and see if she wanted to have a drink before heading home.

I shook my head and whispered, "Too weird."

Every place was probably overbooked with people in crazy costumes. And that begged the question of why I'd driven through my suburb and into the city, miles out of my way. Should I walk solo into a restaurant or bar on the spookiest night of the year?

Truth time. It's been three days since the Sunday hike with Angie, and she hasn't said if she wants to go again this coming weekend. I wanted to go out with her again. Maybe I was barking up the wrong tree. She's just not into me. Or I'm rushing things and about to scare her off permanently.

I liked her, though. Liked her a lot. I'd spend tonight with her if she'd have me, even if that meant pulling her away during the craziest quarter of the year for her kind of work.

I pulled my truck in-between two black SUV's, near the bar where I first met Angie. A few couples in costumes leaned against the brick wall, their quiet conversations blending together. Through the multi-paned glass, I saw an open spot at the bar, so I squeezed past people to the hostess station. When the attractive blonde looked up, I pointed over to the bar, and she nodded.

I slipped between tables quickly so I could get that last spot. Dropping my black jacket onto the back of the stool, I raised an eyebrow at the bartender—less muscular than the one who'd served us over a week ago. "Vodka tonic, thanks."

A survey of the room told me I was definitely the sad case I figured I'd be: an uncostumed guy alone in this bar, wild with noise. The patrons sparkled in mostly orange and black attire. A few couples had assumed disguises I couldn't quite figure out.

I pulled out my phone. I stared at it, debating. I started typing.

Angie, hi. I'm at that place we met last week, having a drink. Would you join me?

I deleted words, started over a couple of times. Finally decided to hit send. Nothing ventured, nothing gained, someone famous once said.

I rubbed a hand over my face, the stubble on my chin creating the soft sound of sandpaper. The bartender set the lowball glass onto a white paper napkin and held a finger up. "Tab or pay now?"

"Tab," I responded, hopeful. My car was parked and I'm here now, no rush to go anywhere. And eager for an Angie date. I really wanted to see her. Now. I ignored my phone, in denial about what my invitation would do to any chances I had with that lovely woman.

The smell of fries and beef from the surrounding tables created a hollow hunger in my stomach. The bartender was too busy to get a menu for me, so I pondered my next steps. My vibrating phone on the dark wood bar jolted me out of my reverie. My heart skipped when I saw the blue dot by Angie's name. Angie. Please be saying yes.

I'm still at work, but will lock up soon. You still there?

Here, as long as you take.

A smiley emoji popped into the text screen. Well, I have a date. A special date on a spooky day.

As the middle of a sad man sandwich at the bar, I doubted my luck in saving a seat for Angie. The bleary-eyed guys on either side of me were there for the long haul. I slipped around the bar as a couple started to move away, thankful yet again to that little arrow-shooting angel, Cupid, who was looking out for me. I surveyed the restaurant, but not a soul was dressed in a diaper carrying a bow-and-arrow.

"May I have two menus, please?" The bartender pulled menus off the bar in front of other customers and brought them over.

"Thanks, man."

My phone vibrated.

On my way.

I pumped a fist in the air, prompting a gray-haired woman nearby to glare at me. She sported a sequined eye mask and stirred her cocktail with a painted finger. Definitely single, I thought unkindly.

Even with my back to the door, I figured Angie would find me without me waving her down. Hopefully, I'd made enough of an impression she'd recognize the back of my head. I gave her ten minutes, then started glancing over my shoulder, probably looking like I had a nervous tick to the lady two stools down who kept glancing over at me.

It hit me that maybe I knew her from somewhere, so I nodded. She slid off her stool, speaking to the gentleman beside her about her purse. To watch it, I guessed.

"Brian?"

"Yeah?" I say it like a question, sorta like "who's asking" without being overtly rude. My parents taught me better than that.

She stuck out a hand and said, "Katrina Spelling. We met at an interview."

"Oh, right." I did actually remember her applying for a job at the plant. She was fairly popular with the interview panel, given her blonde hair and deep blue eyes. She was tall, too. Tall enough that she was eye-level with me beside the bar.

Out of the corner of my eye, I saw Angie enter the restaurant, and I realized that Katrina was still holding my hand. Or was I the one who hadn't let go? I dropped it like a hot potato and waved Angie over.

"My date's here. Nice seeing you again, Katrina."

Katrina backed away with a wounded look. I didn't have time to evaluate the situation because suddenly I was looking downward at my beautiful date in a bright red jacket.

"Here," I said as I slid off the barstool, swiftly draping her jacket over the stool beside mine. "It's great to see you."

"Well, I was a little surprised, but glad I could make it work."

"Surprised?"

"Halloween, last minute."

I cringed inside, castigating myself for creating the whole awkward scenario. "Sorry, I just—"

"Oh, no, don't apologize. I'm sorry. I didn't mean it that way. I literally cannot remember the last time I had a date on Halloween. Who is that woman in the mirror? I ask myself."

"A beautiful woman is who you are."

Angie blushed and looked away, her eyes dropping to the menu on the bar in front of her.

"Have you had dinner? Others are eating at the bar. I doubt we could get a —"

"I'm starved. We were so busy I only had a protein bar around noon, and that's it. But you shouldn't—"

"I planned to eat here, so this is great. And with a perfect dinner companion. A win."

She smiled as she looked up at me. Her dark eyes sparkled, assuring me that she was happy to be there.

"I appreciate you thinking of me."

You're all I think about, I wanted to say, but realized I should back off embarrassing her with too many compliments. Last thing any guy needs is to come off creepy.

While she skimmed the menu, I studied her profile. I scanned my menu, and feeling her gaze on me, I snuck a sideways glance and smirked for her benefit.

"Who's the blonde?"

"The blonde?"

Angie nodded down the bar toward Katrina. I stuttered while searching for the right words. I couldn't mention the job interview because of HR rules, but there was no good lie either.

"She, um..."

"Hey no biggie, we all have exes."

"No, no. She's not an ex. I met her at, uh, a work thing. While back. I didn't even recognize her at first." I sounded defensive, guilty perhaps, and for what?

Angie giggled.

"What's that for?"

"Brian and the blondes." Angie stirred her gin and tonic with a black-and-white-striped cocktail straw.

"The blondes? Plural?" Then I remembered the Kayla thing.

She shrugged. "Forget I said anything. I think I'll have the steak salad like last time."

"Changing the subject. Interesting."

"Why's it interesting? It's your problem, not mine."

"Problem?"

Angie tapped my arm with her knuckles, a mocking fist. "Think we should order? In case they have to go kill the cow for our steak."

"Absolutely." I looked her in the eye, long enough to make her squirm. "And for the record, I'm into dark-eyed, dark-haired beauties."

"Ha, right."

I slung my arm across the back of her chair and leaned close to whisper into her ear, her soft curls tickling my nose. "Listen, you should have not a single doubt that I'm into a certain dark-haired beauty right here."

She turned to look at me, but her gaze slipped to my left, down the bar, then back.

"You don't have to say those things. I know I'm not like Kayla or her." She gestured in Katrina's direction.

"You are definitely not. That's a positive. Okay?"

She nodded slightly.

"Okay?" I repeated firmly.

"K."

I signaled the bartender, who took our dinner orders. It felt strangely intimate that we ordered the same meal as last time.

"We're not done discussing you."

"We're not? What else do you need to say other than I'm a gorgeous brunette?"

"That's the ticket. Positivity." I held up my glass, so she clinked hers against it.

"It's just our third date and you're..." She shook her head.

"I'm what? Into you? What's wrong with that?"

She shook her head again.

"You don't believe me," I muttered.

"I mean... well, yeah, I want to. My track record isn't so great."

"Same."

Her frowning gaze cut me in two. "Women literally throw themselves at you." Her snicker didn't sound kind.

"Not all of them." I quirked an eyebrow at her and she was charitable enough to laugh at my silly joke at her expense. "And, by the way, women do not throw themselves at me."

"You're sweet and friendly, which convinces you that is how other people—especially women—are responding to you. But the women—they are not being friendly, they're being flirty."

"Flirty, huh? We shall see if you can be my flirty girl someday."

"Your flirty girl? Oh, brother." She laughed, and I thought I'd enjoy getting used to that throaty sound.

She looked relieved when our food arrived. A welcome interruption to cover her discomfort with my affection. Sitting side by side rather than across from each other made for a more relaxed conversation. We talked and chuckled through dinner and then the bartender stood in front of us asking about dessert and clearing our plates.

"You have a special Halloween dessert tonight?" I asked the bartender.

The bartender described a chocolate lava cake, and I gave him a thumbs-up.

"Noooo." Angie groaned.

"Two forks so we can share. You know you want some."

"I'm a sucker for chocolate."

"What else excites you?"

"Nope, not going there. Too tired to think."

"Fair enough. I've asked a lot already."

In the dark of night, I wasn't about to let a beautiful lady walk alone to her car, and Angie accepted my argument. Her store was two blocks away, and we walked past her storefront on the way to the parking lot.

"Beautiful windows. I'm impressed."

"Thank you."

"You designed them?"

"Yes, I did. Tomorrow will be crazy, taking down all the spiders and witches to make room for more Thanksgiving and tons of Christmas. Yes, we too throw all the holidays together in the store. Unavoidable this time of year."

"Wow. I guess you ping-pong between every holiday. Do you have a favorite?"

"That's easy. Christmas."

"Me too."

"What do you like best?" She turned around and walked backward in front of me. A smile played around her lips.

"Family time? And the tree, always the tree. Which I'll have to work on this year in my new place."

"I love a big fat Christmas one. My parents always find the best tree every year."

"Here we are." I pointed to the parking lot, overwhelmed by a sense of loneliness because we were about to part. Her tiny red car was parked up against the brick wall of the building, with a sign that read, "MCM Manager Parking" and I'm impressed again.

"I haven't committed to hiking on Sunday, I'm sorry. Have you seen the forecast?"

I chuckled because the TV weather experts were calling for showers. She's not wrong that hiking when it's wet isn't optimal. Still, I love it.

"Besides...," she continued. "Um, well, I won't be done moving inventory. We're switching holidays and..."

I held up a hand. "I have an offer."

"An offer?"

"Yeah, if you need to work at your store on Sunday, I'll come and help."

"Oh heavens, no, I can't ask you to do that."

"Did you ask? No. I'm just offering so I can hang out with you."

"And you can avoid Kayla. A win, right?" She grinned at me. How did she perceive how uncomfortable that Kayla thing was for me?

I waved her words away. "Not even a consideration. I'm a grown man."

"Yeah." Her tone doubtful.

I felt disrespected, a little, but couldn't I allow her some fun at my expense like I'd done to her earlier? We were comfortable teasing each other. That's good, and I sensed something significant developing.

Silence mixed with the fog of our breath. Angie turned to her car as its headlights flashed and the lock chirped.

"Angie."

She spun back around, her face tilted upwards. I stepped closer, excited that we're about to end the night magically. Her lips were soft against mine, and as I moved my hand toward her shoulder, she pulled back. Then, too swiftly, she opened her car door and slid behind the wheel.

"Thank you for the surprise invitation. I'm glad you reached out."

"And Sunday?"

"Text me."

I confess my disappointment. As usual, I'd let my imagination run away when she agreed to meet me at the restaurant. We barely knew each other, but a lot had happened in the ten days since we met for that first drink.

Things were moving in the right direction, but I had to slow down the train in my brain. If I wasn't careful, Angie and I would get knocked off the track before we got close to a desirable destination.

Whatever that might be.

Chapter 8

Angie

IN MY BEDROOM, I flipped the music to Coltrane's "My Favorite Things" because he'd mentioned family at Christmas. My heart had soared in that moment. It's always been hard for me to connect with a guy who wasn't close to his family or couldn't see value in the special times that only a family offers.

Besides, he'd also kissed me, one of my most favorite things. Not that I'm going to tell him any time soon how much I really, really enjoy kissing. We needed more time to know each other, but I didn't mind that sweet little kiss. A Halloween, not-spooky surprise, though I have to admit I'd kind of invited it. Hoped for it, honestly. The minute I got his text, I hoped something magical would happen.

Coltrane's styling on the soprano saxophone zinged through me as the perfect accompaniment to the lingering memory of the evening. I sat at the bar with Brian for nearly three hours, time whizzing by while we talked about work and family.

Brian saw me, the real me. The way he looked at me was so focused and appreciative. I made him happy somehow. Wow, how do I possibly believe any of those random musings? I didn't know my own self, let alone what made me or another person happy. Suddenly, I was sucking the joy out of my head, and I should have stopped being so negative.

The clock said ten o'clock, far too late to call Sylvie. Lucky little Sylvie. Got her a great guy, and the promise of happily ever after. Sigh. I had so many questions, but they'd have to wait.

When Brian talked about his friends, I had to just listen. No marvelous stories could I offer about hanging out with the gals. As more of the store's responsibilities fell upon me, I'd developed the bad habit of saying "no" whenever someone asked me to go out dancing or whatever. After a ten-hour day at the mercantile, going home tended to be the main objective. I probably spent more time with Sylvie on the phone than anyone else I knew here in Birmingham. I've wondered, though, if we'd see each other much if she still lived in Alabama.

I miss my friend terribly, but she has flown the coop, and she's roosting elsewhere. And thriving. Besides being brilliant, Sylvie's beautiful and so sweet. We have history and I wouldn't trade thirty minutes with a local girlfriend for a single minute on the phone with Sylvie.

When I'd pulled into the driveway ten minutes ago, I was near tears from missing her. All the house lights were out, but Dad or Mom had left the porch light on for me. A fleeting thought reminded me instantly of a hotel commercial.

My parents had lived in this house since before I was born. Before that, they'd lived on the other side of the city, a lot further away from the business. Moving to this three-bedroom house with its brick facade and black-and-white painted trim had been significant for them. Mom was pregnant, and they were already considering living in a better school district. Fortunate for me in many ways, but for me in the long-run it meant I got to meet Sylvie and her family decades ago. Her momma is seriously cool, and very glamorous with so much blonde hair. That it's still teased up eighties-style means nothing, other than she's always reminded me of a movie star. No wonder Mr. Bradley still looked so in love with her.

Not that Sylvie saw it. I'd only looked through a window into their lives, but she'd seen things up close and personal. I've heard the stories, but I'm just gonna believe what I want to about an enduring love for the Bradley parents. I wondered, though, how that'd all play out during a stressful wedding season for them.

Well, we shall see, won't we?

My dad's soft snores drifted through their closed door down the hall from my room. I smiled, understanding Mom's occasional complaints. But she hadn't banished Dad to the third bedroom—their marriage meant more than a good night's sleep, I figured.

After changing into pajamas and brushing my teeth, I climbed into bed. Flat on my back, my heart skipped a beat, and a tight breath left my lungs. I have another freaking date tomorrow.

"Oh no," I moaned, throwing an arm across my eyes in a futile attempt to shut off the vision of a confused Angie having a drink with Jake. How did I go from zero to two dates in a single workweek? I should have felt like an empowered, desirable woman, but I'd never experienced such feelings. Ever.

But perhaps I'd gotten close to feeling slightly desirable that night—with Brian. He was incredibly attentive, and his compliments had made me blush from the inside out, warming me like a fuzzy blanket. I could wrap myself up inside his words, and his sexy and admiring gaze.

Wait, sexy? Was I really thinking about Brian being sexy after only three dates? I'd truly gotten out of practice and out of touch with my feelings. And feelings have been my operational base since I was about twelve years old. That's as far back as I can remember getting myself worked up about something. And being overly dramatic about it, that is. That's when my anxiety hit a high gear and I started seeing a therapist.

Brian and I had chemistry, obviously. But what's the rush?

How I wished I could talk to Sylvie. I checked my phone for the time. Midnight. The screen's glare lit up the pale bedsheet that covered me. I opened the messaging app to type a message.

Hey girlfriend, please call me in the morning if you can.

I closed my eyes, the phone resting on my abdomen. The phone's buzzing interrupted my deep breathing exercise, and I jumped. The phone bounced from the bed to the floor.

"Shoot." I cringed, hoping my parents didn't hear the carpet-muffled fall. of my cell phone.

Scooping it up, I was shocked to see a reply from Sylvie. Sylvie was awake at midnight—never happened.

Hey, what's up? Everything okay?

Not okay, nothing's okay, but it'll wait till the morning. Why are you awake?

Too excited to sleep. Wedding stuff running through my brain.

Pete there?

Absolutely not. He's waiting like a good boy.

"Good grief." I rolled my eyes in the dark about Sylvie's virginal goals.

My phone started ringing, the screen black with red and green buttons, and Sylvie's name glowing in white.

"Much better, but hang on a sec."

"What for?"

"Sleeping parents. Let me get downstairs." Sylvie had no idea what it's like to live with parents when you're in your thirties. Awesome or awful, depending on the day.

"Okay," she whispered, which made me giggle again.

"Tell me about your day," I whispered from the kitchen, lit only by the glow of the open refrigerator. Who was I kidding? I didn't need a thing to eat, not after that gorgeous lava cake. Or drink. I shut the door, glass bottles clanging against each other inside the door.

"Oh, it was pretty wonderful," Sylvie practically sang it.

"It is wonderful. You're getting married. Eek!"

"True. But..."

"But what? Aren't you excited?"

"Excited, yes. What do I do with myself until December twenty-second?"

"Give yourself a break. Plus, your bridal shower is in two weeks."

"Momma is making me a little nuts. I am so glad you agreed to run interference."

"Running interference. Such fun."

"She shared about the flower problem. Is that why you wanted to talk?"

"No. That flower thing got fixed. It was totally my mistake. I've got way too much on my plate. I arrived home late and wanted to talk to my dearest friend."

"I'm so sorry, Ang. I owe you big time for asking so much of you at your busiest time of year."

I sighed and plopped down in my dad's recliner, it's leather cold on my skin, even through my cotton pajamas.

"I had a date tonight. Or last night, that is. On Halloween. Weird, huh? My first ever spooky date, haha."

"Not weird. Who'd you go out with?"

"Brian."

"The hiking guy?"

"Yup. He randomly texted me as I was closing up. He was at the bar where we first met. So I met him there."

"Wow. Isn't that like three dates in less than two weeks? That may be a world record or something."

"I doubt it's a world record, but it's an Angie record, for sure."

"Then what's wrong?"

"I like him."

"That's good! What's really goin' on, Ang?"

"I have a date tomorrow, I mean, tonight with Jake! I'm no good at this dating around thing."

"Well, for one, you haven't really tried it. You might like the variety and… you know." She chuckled.

"Variety? That might be overrated. And exhausting. Different guys two nights in a row. Well, it seems… I dunno."

"It's whatever. Just go with it. Where's the bossy Angie who told me how to go after Pete a mere ten months ago?"

"That Angie is on vacation because of extreme confusion. It's a very private one. A personal retreat, so to speak." I ran a hand through my hair and laughed. Sylvie laughed with me.

"Why do I get the sense something else is going on?"

I sighed, then moaned, and fake cried—so dramatic. I was back in high school, crying over a boy with my best friend. Believe me, boy-tears were a real thing back then. "Oh Sylvie, he's just… he's pretty awesome, and he obviously likes me."

"Definitely, for sure."

"He said he's into me," I whispered the last three words.

"Oh my, oh my, Angie, my friend, that is real. I mean, he must be for real. I mean, it sounds like it, right?"

"Yeah," I barely choked out the word. My throat was tight with anxiety.

"Deep breaths," Sylvie whispered. So I stood and stretched my free hand above my head, breathing in through my nose, out through my mouth.

"I wonder if I'm projecting on him."

"Meaning?"

"Well, I'm thirty-two and experiencing the pull to get out of my parents' house and start a life on my own. I want to find someone to share my life with, like you have. Desperation's gotten hold of me for some reason, possibly given I've had such a long, dry spell in my love life."

"And you've decided he may be thinking similar things? Does he live at home still?"

"He actually bought a condo a year ago, over in Chelsea. His family's in Tuscaloosa."

"Well... I don't know what to say. Take it one day at a time. Don't stress."

"Uh, who're you talkin' to? I have stressing-out down to an art form!"

"True. Maybe helping me with the wedding will distract you from all these questions you have."

"Possibly. I need a distraction. I almost forgot, I have more news. When I made a work excuse to avoid freezing my butt off in the woods this Sunday, Brian offered to help me at the store."

"Giving up a hike for you. That's significant, don't you think?"

"Yeah," I choked out that word again. I inhaled noisily, which prompted Sylvie to giggle.

"Oh Ang, I'm sorry, but I'm laughing with you. You're gonna be okay. Just enjoy the ride to love." Sylvie sang the love phrase, and I rolled my eyes. Love had surely changed my friend.

"Oh, good lord."

We both chuckled. Then I heard Sylvie yawn.

"I need to let you get to bed. Sweet dreams, bride-to-be."

"Thanks. I'm so glad we're friends."

I could hear the smile wrapped around gratitude across the hundreds of miles between us. Her warmth and friendship hugged me like a cocoon.

"Me too. I'll keep the dating news regular and entertaining, ha-ha. Good night, Sylvie."

"Night night."

I tossed the phone onto my dad's chair and stretched tall with my hands above my head. I rolled my head from side to side, then pressed my chin into my chest, sensing the taut muscles soften with each stretch. My anti-anxiety exercises kept me sane, and I surely needed more sanity in my life. My love life was making me crazy. So crazy, I literally forgot to tell Sylvie that I got kissed too.

My phone lit up and dinged with another text. Really, Sylvie, still can't sleep? But it wasn't my friend after all.

Hey, thanks for meeting up tonight! Apologies again for the last minute.

He'd punctuated it with the smiley face with red heart eyes.

Oh, Brian, you silly man. I silenced the phone and headed back upstairs. Slipping between silky soft cotton sheets, I smiled about my life, about my new admirer. Don't know how it happened, but I slid away into a dreamless sleep that lasted until I smelled the rich dark coffee my parents made every morning.

It'd been a while since I'd lost myself over a guy, but the past couple of weeks of Brian dreams had disturbed all my life rhythms — work, sleep, eating.

At work, I'd stared unseeing out the window or at the computer screen. An interruption by Vanessa sent me bouncing startled out of my chair. I'd taken to eating banged up boxes of chocolate candy, ones we couldn't sell. My teeth hurt from so much sugar. And I was tired. Prior to last night, I'd chased fuzzy white sheep around my ceiling for a week's worth of nights.

I suppose talking to Sylvie had helped me get over my issues enough to get some rest and reset my overall well-being. At the store, the switchover of holiday merchandise forced me into a hyper-focused mode that lasted beyond my usual lunchtime. Vanessa and I piled some of the Halloween leftovers in the back room for our college helper to pack in the afternoon. Half of the leftovers were food-related and considered perishable and got moved to a half-off sale table in the back corner. Gotta make the customers walk past the full-price stuff before they're allowed to touch the bargains!

"You're on a roll. What's got into you?" Vanessa asked me while we ate our lunches in my office. It was past two, so we took advantage of the lull in customer traffic to eat.

"You want these chocolates?" I pulled a shiny orange box out of the bottom desk drawer, my hiding place for treats. A protein bar sat alone in the far back.

"Oh, gosh no. I'm over it," she replied with a laugh and a wave of her hand. She nodded when I held the box over the trashcan and raised my eyebrows. *Clunk.*

I closed my eyes and took a deep breath, the aroma of my chicken noodle soup warming my senses.

"Thank goodness we're done with candy corn season."

"Have you seen the foil-wrapped Santa bars in the back room?"

"I know, I know, and there are so many more candies for the upcoming season. I like your idea of a little holiday decor slowdown between Halloween and the next two months of insanity."

"Been stressful, for sure. But it's hardly a slowdown. I'm gonna use the next day or so to plan out the layout for the new vendors we're stocking. And I still need your eyes and skill."

She waved a hand, dismissing the compliment. I did need her, even if only I realized it.

"And you seem to have a private life. For a change." Vanessa smirked. "I guess that's what's gotten into you?"

"Maybe. I had a last-minute dinner last night. Drink date tonight."

"Same guy?"

"Um. How do I explain this—" I looked down at my soup, struggling with the words to describe my complete terror about dating around like a female Don Juan. Ha, who am I kidding? I'm nothing like a man magnet, even though I felt a bit like Jezebel. Seeing someone else while I was possibly falling for Brian? What was I thinking? Truth was, I couldn't think straight at all when Brian's shimmery blue eyes danced around my head.

Vanessa's warm brown eyes took me in. Her flawless dark skin needed no makeup, but I detected a shimmer of peach powder on her high cheekbones. Mascara thickened her already long, full eyelashes. I was so jealous.

"No need to explain nothin'." She laid a hand on my arm.

The words came out in a rush—how I'd ventured online and had three dates with the same guy in no time at all, and another guy tonight. I was so confused and crazy-sounding, but Vanessa just nodded as she listened to my tale of joy and woe.

"Sounds like good times."

"Good times? I'm dying here."

She shook her head. "Enjoy, enjoy. That's what you're supposed to do at your age. You might have Mr. Right in your midst."

Mr. Right. Yeah. A girl must dream.

"Well, maybe so. That's that then. I guess we should finish collecting the sparkling jack-o'-lanterns from the windows. Ready?"

Jake and I agreed to meet at a bar across the city, near the restaurant he managed. I'd have preferred to stay closer to my store, but was relieved to avoid the risk of running into Brian. See, this is why I'm not good at playing the field. I already felt like I'm sneaking around and I'm not even in a committed relationship. And I won't ever get into one if I'm stringing two guys along.

But am I? What if they're stringing me along, seeing someone else too? What if I end up alone again when I get caught? I shook off the troubling thoughts and drove across town.

I arrived before Jake. The bar area was loud and crowded. Isn't it just Thursday? What's up with that?

My phone vibrated in my pink leather purse, and I figured Jake was running late. Like the first time, I must add.

Brian.

Oh goodness, I never replied to his midnight text. Plum forgot. What to do? I peeked out the door and didn't see Jake coming, so I started texting an apology. He was kindly checking up on me.

Frowning at my phone, I failed to notice the opening door as it swung toward me. The phone clattered on the black and white tile floor and slid under a plant stand.

"Oh!"

I looked down, then up to find myself staring at Jake's grinning face.

"Sorry, I'm late, love."

Love?

"My phone." I squatted beside the wooden stand and walked my fingers under it till I could snatch the stupid escapee.

Jake was in conversation with the hostess—must they all be blonde—who grabbed two red leatherette menus and walked us to a table smack dab in the middle of the restaurant. I looked around, hoping to find a booth to move to. Nothing. I rolled my eyes as I pulled out my chair.

"Bad day, huh?"

Observant. Points for Jake. But I waved off the question. "An okay day."

I thought we were meeting for drinks, but apparently dinner was on the agenda. As he chatted about a recalcitrant employee, I slipped my feet out of my pointy pink flats to relieve my pinched toes. After a grueling two hours of discussing management dilemmas *again*, I wandered to my car alone. Jake had parked in the opposite direction, so I happily declined his offer to walk me, even though I was in a strange part of town in the dark. He didn't seem terribly disappointed that I nixed spending a little more time with him.

Instead of choosing some jazz tunes, I hit some buttons on my phone and soon Sylvie's voice was floating through my speakers. Yay, technology! She talked me home and then while I got into my pajamas. She convinced me to text Brian about helping at work on Sunday. And that reminded me to finish texting him back. I might not make a reliable girlfriend, he could justifiably decide.

Girlfriend?

Chapter 9

Brian

"WHAT DOES IT MEAN if a girl doesn't answer a text?"

My brother, John, scoffed. "I'm supposed to know that?"

I sighed as I fell against the pillows on my bed. All day at work, I'd kept an eye on my phone, hoping Angie would answer the text I sent in the early hours. Perhaps that was the problem. I'd intruded into some private space she wanted to protect—the time she was asleep.

"John, I like her. She's special."

"Well, be patient. Let things play out."

I rolled my eyes. Easy for him to say, old married dude. "It's just—"

"Brother Brian, I get it. I think I do anyway. But come on. Does she have a job? Responsibilities? Give her a break."

"Fine. Fine. I'm acting fifteen, I hear ya."

John chuckled. "I don't recall you stressing about girls back then. They just threw themselves at you. Never figured out why."

"Charm and personality."

"Mom passed all her dark good looks on to you. Ryan and I are just chopped liver."

"Ah come on," I whined a bit, slightly embarrassed. John's version was not how I remembered things, but after hiking buddy Mike pointed out my cluelessness, well... it's been on my mind. Even Angie had poked fun.

"Listen, you're just getting acquainted. Patience, brother."

"Ah, look at you being all poetic."

"On that note, I gotta scoot. The wifey's looking at me—my turn to put the kiddos to bed."

"Wish I was there. I love putting those critters to bed. 'One more story, Uncle Brian!'"

"Yeah, it's all fun and games for the uncles. Night, man."

"Thanks, John, for listening."

"Any time. You know that."

I sure did. John had turned out to be a pretty decent older brother. Going through a few recovery programs had improved his attitude toward people. Toward pretty much everything, truthfully.

I checked my phone for any new texts and noted the late hour. Ten o'clock, nearly twenty-four hours since I messaged Angie, then that embarrassing check-in text around dinner time. Had I gone into the creep zone? I didn't believe that. I've been clear about how I feel about her. Radio silence was not a pleasant sound, so I filled the air with the staccato noise of popping corn. A bit late for a snack, but I couldn't head to bed yet. Where was she? Was she okay?

I stretched out on my gray leather sectional sofa, feet crossed, and a red plastic bowl of buttery popcorn resting on my stomach. The smooth white ceiling provided no answers to the question of Angie's silence. But it made for a good screen to replay the movie of our last date.

I must have dozed off, the musical ding of my phone jolting me upward, the popcorn bowl falling upside down on the hardwood floor. Crap! Forgetting about the phone momentarily, I found the broom and dustpan in the hall closet and started cleaning up. The phone dinged again. Practicing the patience John advocated, I dumped popcorn into the trash and returned the cleaning tools to the closet.

My heartbeat skipped like popcorn jumping in an oil-slicked pan as I lifted the phone. The phone woke in my hand, revealing my lock screen photo of a forest floor. The notification bar announced a text from Angie. Hallelujah! My fingers stumbled too much in my excited rush to read her reply. She's okay. I was grateful to learn.

Sorry I didn't reply to your late night text. The day got away from me. Your next text got lost in crazy dinner stuff. I'm really sorry.

I wiped my hand down my face, exhaling a relieved breath. Three dots appeared on the screen, and I contemplated waiting to see what else she'd say. Instead, I jumped in.

My offer still stands to help you on Sunday. Still planning to do store work?

I wasn't ignoring you. I feel so badly.

She was typing a text while I was. Our eagerness to talk to each other warmed me.

Yes, I should be working in the stockroom on Sunday. Will have to see how tomorrow and Saturday go.

And I can help?

I'd like that a lot. Let's plan for it.

I fist-pumped the air. I had a date. Well, sort of. I'd take it. Truth? I'd take anything if it meant hanging out with Angie, enjoying the intoxicating scent of her shampoo or perfume. When she looked straight at me, into my eyes, I ached with emotion. The feeling was indescribable at this early point in our relationship—a stage I planned on getting us through quickly as I worked my charm.

With the unanswered text problem gone, I could go to bed. I needed a good night's sleep as I had the lead presentation at a big meeting in the morning.

As I pulled the sheet around my shoulders, I had the most childish thought. Three more sleeps. Then I'd see

Angie again with her sparkling brown eyes and mischievous smile.

Like a kid at Christmas.

Magic City Mercantile's windows held no shimmer. Gone were the orange lights and shiny witch hats, an unbelievable transformation in a few days. They were basically undecorated—where was Christmas? I stared past the jarred candles and fall leaves and into the store, searching for movement to tell me that Angie was ready. I had parked my truck beside her car in the lot around the corner, so I knew she was there. But was she ready to see me? I'd started doubting this thing—this relationship—as soon as I got way too excited about seeing Angie on a Sunday afternoon for such mundane work.

A light came on near the front of the store. When I rapped on the etched glass with a knuckle, I was rewarded with movement, and the shape of Angie, backlit by a golden glimmer, coming through a doorway.

The happy notes of her voice competed with the bells chiming above the door as she opened it. I didn't know how she stood that sound constantly every day.

"Hi. You made it!" Angie rubbed her palms down her jeans as she flashed a bright smile.

"Hey." I didn't know what else to say. I'm rarely mute, but going to Angie's business on a weekend to do actual work prompted an awkwardness the moment I stepped into that retail space filled with shelves, tables, and lighting everywhere.

We headed toward a lighted doorway, Angie a study in motion, walking ahead of me, talking with her hand. A laugh escaped her lips, and I wasn't sure what was funny. I must have missed something.

We entered the brightly lighted space, where I witnessed a mess. She'd call it an organized mess, no doubt. It's what Marcia at work called her desk. On the right side of the old wooden desk, scarred from years of bearing an office manager's thoughts and feelings, sat a laptop. A wireless mouse rested on a mousepad decorated with what looked like mice in Santa hats. The other half of the desk featured piles of manila folders and scattered papers.

"Welcome to my world," Angie announced with arms spread wide. She sighed and plopped into a black office chair, which scooted backward a few inches. She waved to the chair in front of me. "Let's strategize."

She wanted strategy? Hmm, I wasn't sure how helpful I would be having never ever worked in a store. I'd earned money in the summers as a lifeguard and had to make it stretch so I could play football and baseball in high school and focus on my studies in college.

"Okay? What do you want me to do?"

Angie hopped up, skimmed past me, and out the door. "Lemme give you the tour. Two cents worth."

I chuckled, wondering what we'd accomplish if she was this scattered all the time. Would we be here all day? I'd arrived at ten on the dot, unsure of the day's agenda. Open to new experiences: my pep-talk that morning. I trusted Angie to orient me to the unaccustomed work.

The store itself kept going and going, broken into sections of walls decorated with pictures, wreaths, and garlands. I thought that's what those long flowery things were. Past any wall we entered a themed space — a holiday, the beach, sale merchandise. One section featured a wall with candles displayed almost to the ceiling. Racks of tea towels carried out each space's theme.

"How do you keep up with all this stuff? Man, it's so much!"

"Ten years ago, when I got out of college, I convinced my parents...well, mainly Dad, to computerize everything. I mean everything. I had to learn the software, set up the system, all of it."

She tapped the side of her forehead. "It's all up here, so I'm indispensable."

"I'm sure you already were. But what if you got sick?"

She rolled her eyes and smiled ruefully. "That cannot happen."

"Really?"

"No, not really. I've trained Vanessa, our assistant manager, on the system. She knows the point-of-sale system better than me. She helps way more customers than I do. And I rely on her to train our part-timers. Still, I do need someone else to understand the system and everything else I do." She shrugged and turned toward a set of gray double doors, black-rimmed windows set about five feet up. A white-and-red "Employees Only" sign stuck to the right-hand door.

"And this is my dad's domain."

"He does this by himself? Keeps it organized?"

"And unpacks boxes, sweeps floors, and unloads trucks. He's getting too old for it."

I walked to the other side of a large wooden table and faced her. "This is a lot. Wow! I'm impressed you have all of this place under control."

A pained noise escaped her lips.

I frowned, watching her gather her emotions. Angie wanted to talk, I could tell. And then she surprised me more.

Angie stuck her arms straight out and wiggled her fingers. Her breathing came in deep gulps, eyes closed, thick lashes on her cheeks. Out of respect, I stayed still.

Her eyes flickered open. She stared at me briefly before dropping her eyes to the table between us.

"Sorry 'bout that. My anxiety exercise."

"Better?"

She nodded and smiled.

"Weird, huh? Go ahead, you can say it."

"Nah. You're brave, letting me in like this."

"Thank you. It was an anxiety attack. Quick and painless, thank goodness."

I shrugged and walked around the table to her. "I'm here to help you. I came to help in the store, but if I help you some other way, it's all good. Right?"

She lifted her eyes to mine, fear mingling with embarrassment in them.

"What's it like when you get those... um... attacks? I mean, only if you want to share."

"Well." She let out a sigh and considered it. "Sometimes I get cold, or I break into a sweat. Sometimes both. My chest gets tight, and it's hard to breathe. I have to fight against the tightness a little to do the deep breathing, but that's what helps me the most. Even more than meds. I'm not taking anything now. I'm sure that's a relief to you."

"Why would that be a relief?"

"Oh, you know, the girl you're seeing isn't on mental health drugs." She turned away. Embarrassed, I assumed.

"Thanks for telling me that. Like I said, I will happily help you with whatever."

A huge white cat hopped onto the long center table, and I jumped.

"You don't like cats?"

"No. Yeah, they're fine. It just scared the mess out of me."

We both chuckled.

She stroked the cat's head. "This here is Colin."

She named a cat Colin? Interesting. And a bit weird. The cat looked like a Tinkerbell to me.

"I found him in the park across the street about twelve years ago. He was a wild one, about a year old, we estimated. Feral indeed."

"Huh."

"Yep. I started feeding him, and he became a fixture in the stockroom. Eventually, he got brave enough to mix it up with the customers." She giggled. "Sometimes, he peeks out from under a tablecloth and shocks someone. But it's usually okay."

"So we have Colin, the feral cat? I sense a wordplay here."

"Smart. Yes, one of my favorite actors."

"Does he meow with an English accent?"

"Irish, you mean. Different Colin." She shook her head in mock disgust, which only made me laugh harder.

"But I went back to college after that summer, and my parents pledged to look after him. Of course, I had to threaten that I'd never return to the store if anything happened to him. They took it to heart, and now he's a family member here at the store."

I stroked my hand down his spine. "He's a chunky fella."

"Hey. Not nice."

"Sorry. I'm glad I'm here to meet your cat."

"I'm glad you're here too. Truly I am."

"Me too. Ready to put me to work?"

"Ah, yes, we should get to it. I kinda already have a strategy in mind, to be honest. We took one day's break before hauling out most of the holly, so to speak. But I'm thinking there's something you can help me with."

I bowed. "At your service, my lady."

Angie laughed and shook her head. "Oh brother. Now, that... that is weird!"

"Ha ha."

"Come on. We store the Christmas trees in another space. My dad has been buying up property on this block for many years. We still barely use half of it. I'm not sure what his goal is."

"Maybe you should ask."

"Yeah, maybe."

She continued to walk ahead of me, her gray collegiate sweatshirt baggy on her slight frame. Her jeans fit perfectly, definitely not baggy. Nice.

"My parents are going to leave all this to me. Only me, the only kid. It's a lot. I'd like a little more say sooner rather than later, but too often I get the feeling that I need to 'stay in my lane' and I hate that."

"Well, I can't comment. But I will say that I sort of understand how you would feel if you have no authority."

"And here we are." Angie slid open a large wooden slab on iron rollers. Stepping through the opening, I turned slowly, drawn to a dim light fighting to get through the somewhat creepy blackness. Up high, twenty or thirty feet up, I found the source: an oblong stained-glass window made of red and gold geometric panes. Angie came up beside me with a black flashlight so long it resembled a police nightstick. When I motioned to it, she handed it to me. I flicked the light over the window and below it. Double doors with huge iron handles loomed like the gateway to a castle.

"Lights?"

"Um, I dunno. Dad and Otis usually come in here and get the trees. I've always depended on the light from this back hall."

I flicked the beam around the majestic doors and found switches. A modernization that didn't fit what we'd glimpsed so far. Light flickered overhead, slightly delayed after I flipped the switches upward.

"Wow," Angie whispered beside me, her head tilted back.

"Wow is right. Those are some impressive chandeliers. You've never noticed them?"

"Nuh-uh."

"It's like a chapel."

"A chapel?" Angie's voice held tentative doubt. "Really?"

"Definitely. Check out those doors and the stained glass. The glass needs a serious clean."

"It all does. Hey, look at the walls. The wood looks ancient."

I studied the roughhewn wood panels on each of the side walls. The wall that housed the doors and the back wall looked a bit like stucco or plaster, a stunning creamy texture. I'd need more light, and more expertise to be sure.

"This molding, the higher chair rail... and man, the texture of it." I looked at Angie. "I swear, this must've been a chapel at some point. There's no cross, but what else might it have been?"

"Yeah. Possibly. But what does it matter?"

"Well. One. It may be a historic place. Two. You could use that to your business advantage. I'm butting in here, but you could use this to Angie's business advantage. Make your mark, put your stamp on the mercantile."

Angie started waving her arms across her body. "Whoa. What're you talking about?"

"Expand the business!" I grinned as I walked closer to her.

Angie shook her head. "That'll never, ever happen. Not in a million years."

"Why not?"

"My parents."

I looked around the grand space and saw possibilities, amazing opportunities. I couldn't believe this incredible room was sitting there, an unrealized dream. Angie's voice brought me back to earth.

"So, let's look at the Christmas trees."

"Sure, tell me what you want me to do."

I'd stated my piece about the chapel room, and truth time: I don't know a single thing about Angie's business or her parents. But I hoped the incredible prospects of this space would percolate in her pretty head.

"Let's start with this tree. But once we get it onto the floor, we'll have to move some tables. And those tables'll have to be unloaded. Geez, what was I thinking?"

"I'm totally ready for this."

Did she eye-roll me?

The hours passed until both of us leaned against the stockroom doors and blew out our breath. I heard her stomach growl first, and mine echoed.

"Lunch?" I asked, hoping for more time with her.

"Um." Her eyes darted around the store, her mind hard at work.

"Come on. Ya gotta eat, Angie."

"Okay, let's try the cafe around the corner."

Yes!

I'm not a bragger by nature, but I killed that lunch date. I had Angie laughing so hard, she acted like an entirely different person. Distance from work and a good guy's attention—a perfect remedy, right?

That store, well, it's a cool place, and it's likely because she's there, but Angie's "cool" factor diminished when we were working in it. I barely recognized her, as time in the store seemed to drain her energy.

That's why I think the "chapel" property could be a game-changer, but it'll have to sit on her brain for a while, I supposed. I'd said my piece. Far be it from me to interfere.

Chapter 10

Angie

"Mom, Dad," I spoke with a confidence that could only be inspired by Brian. I fixed my coffee and joined them at the kitchen table.

"Good morning, dear," my mom said.

"I have a question, an idea. I worked yesterday and wandered into the center storage room. The one where we keep the Christmas trees."

"I thought you wanted to take a break before pointing our customers to Christmas," said my dad as he added cream to his coffee mug.

"I did. I do, I mean, but if you think about it, we already have. When's the last time we didn't start putting up Christmas trees before Halloween? We didn't this year, so if our sales are lower, we'll have to go back to mushing the holidays together like everyone else. Anyway, I wandered in to look at the trees and turned on the lights. And wow."

Awake into the morning hours, I had practiced this conversation and left Brian out of it for now.

"Wow?" Mom asked.

"Yeah, it kinda looks like a chapel. Have you been in there?"

Mom and Dad exchanged a glance.

"What?"

"Honey, what're you getting at?"

"Dad." I blew out an exasperated breath. He was putting out the roadblocks on a street I'd yet to pave.

"A chapel? I don't understand."

"Well, have you turned on the lights? There are three, yes, three, chandeliers hanging from a beautiful ceiling. And the doors onto Mill Street are gorgeous. If we clean the stained glass above them—"

"And do what, dear?" My mother peered over her coffee with a mystified expression.

"I don't know exactly, but I thought we might have a serious discussion about how to exploit that space and all the square footage you've bought to its best advantage. And to ours, to be more precise. What if we branched out?"

I still couldn't believe that Brian's awestruck commentary about the space had kept me awake past midnight. Now, because of that man, cute and smart as he was, I was involved in yet another frustrating business conversation with my parents.

My parents exchanged another glance over their coffee mugs. Are they really letting me run out of leash? I feel like a dog chained in the yard at times, only permitted to go but so far. "Stay in my lane" echoed while I sipped my coffee and let silence settle over the kitchen table. This fight, if that was what it is, was about more than the chapel space. It had a lot to do with my place in the family business. A deeper discussion had been a long time coming—what was Angie's lane? My parents needed to answer that, but instead I got the silent treatment. Wow, seriously wow.

I dropped a slice of whole wheat bread in the toaster and leaned past my mom to get the butter off the table. Adding a slice of bacon, I folded the soft toast into a quick breakfast sandwich. Dad had returned to reading the paper while Mom was scrolling her phone. Honestly, I wanted to leave the kitchen, but if I did, I'd look like a pouty child which wouldn't help my case any.

I pondered all I did at the mercantile. I basically ran the entire front of the store, a large seven-thousand-square-foot retail store, with Vanessa and two part-timers. I've wanted another full-time salesperson, but Dad won't budge. The store had grown in size and sales, but Dad never considered the strain that losing Mom to her volunteering had put on the sales floor. I've been expected to pick up the slack and I have as best I can. Admittedly, Dad's been flexible enough to come out of the stockroom during the busiest seasons, but he needed too much help with the sales software. Though Otis helped him manage the stockroom, he also was not quite full time. Plus, he'd been gone for a month to help his sick mother.

I was burned out, possibly beyond repair. Perhaps they were right, no matter what they thought about the chapel. How could I bite off a new project when the weight of the store already pressed down so heavily on me? Still, I needed some kind of boost to bring me out of this funk.

"All right, time to finish getting ready for work."

"Angie, I'll be in a bit late."

"K, Dad."

Really? I huffed inside my head and ran up the stairs to my bedroom. I nearly slammed the door. Geez.

Angie, since you worked at the store on your only day off, why don't you go in late also? Said no one ever!

I looked through my messy closet for the gold cardigan that would go well with my golden brown ankle boots. The ding of my phone's message app pulled me to my unmade bed. I scanned the room and sighed. My disorderly room was a metaphor for my life.

Good morning, beautiful. Thanks for a fun day.

Fun day working for free? And wasn't he a sweetheart calling me beautiful? He kinda was the perfect definition of a sweetheart. As soon as I locked the front door of the store, Brian had taken my hand and held it all the way to the cafe. He made me laugh my head off for an hour until I had to get back to some store paperwork. We parted at the cafe door without a kiss goodbye. Disappointing. Though we'd shared some incredible moments yesterday, I feared I'd exposed myself too much when I had the panic attack. What if that sent Brian into a panic when time passed?

Happy Monday! I hope you have a good week. Thank you for helping yesterday. You were great.

Ugh. What did I just write? That sounded like a business brushoff, not warm and appreciative.

Three dots swayed on my phone screen. I thought about something sweeter to write—nothing. I was useless at this dating thing.

Hope you have a good week, too. Are you up for hiking this Sunday?

I started to reply when his next message popped in, that lovely blue oval with more good stuff.

Or have dinner one night after work?

Or both?

He was fast on the keyboard. Impressive. We had a late shipment coming one night this week, so I needed to check my calendar. What the heck. Three questions asked and what would I answer?

Both!

I sent the message with two smiling emojis. Two dates with Brian this week would put a strain on the schedule. My library book would be returned soon, unfinished. Brian was the only bright spot in my life.

Which night works best for you? I'm wide open, of course.

I'm running late! The message from Vanessa interrupted me as I read Brian's text.

Headed out now.

Not exactly true, but I'd arrive at the store before ten. Good enough.

I grabbed my purse and headed downstairs. Through the doorway into the kitchen, I saw my parents lingering still over their stupid coffee mugs, so exasperating. I shut the door without saying a word.

Vanessa dropped her bag on the floor beside my desk and grunted. "I hate my cat. Nectar got out this morning, and I had to chase her behind the shrubs in front of my house."

"Look in the mirror." I pointed to the white framed mirror on the back of my door.

"Oh gosh," Vanessa groaned as she pulled boxwood leaves from her hair. "That explains the weird look I got at the coffee shop."

I giggled.

"Hey, come with me a minute?"

"Sure. What's up?"

"Wanna show you something."

"Mysterious." Vanessa hung her coat on a hook behind my office door and followed me.

"I'm gonna lock the door for a minute, in case of early customers. What time is it?"

"Ten oh five."

Silently, we wove through the stockroom and into the space that had me all excited. Vanessa understood my quiet morning routine—I'm not very chatty until noon.

"Stand here," I told her after I pulled open the sliding door. With my phone's flashlight app, I scanned the far wall until I found the switches. Flipping them, I turned to catch Vanessa's expression.

She blinked and scanned the ceiling, then the rest of the room. Her eyes finally landed on the stained glass. The sun wouldn't streak through till after lunch, so it wasn't that impressive.

"Wow."

"Right? What does it remind you of?" I crossed my fingers, figuratively speaking.

"Kinda like a church? What is this space? Does it belong to the store?"

"We've just used this space for Christmas tree storage and storing other big items."

"Wow again. It's pretty, but needs a lot of TLC."

"Yeah."

"Do you want to do something with it?"

"Perhaps, but Mom and Dad..." I shrugged.

Vanessa and I sighed together. Vanessa didn't really take sides, but when I occasionally grumbled out loud, she encouraged me to press on my parents. Just in a mildly suggesting way, as I'm not confident Vanessa would go against my parents. Mom hired her. She was closer to their age than mine.

Vanessa touched my arm. "Give it time."

I'd given my parents ten years since graduation, and they still treated me like a child. I hadn't made much headway since I got the computerization project completed. That had been a heavy lift for everyone, so I can't say they haven't listened to me at all. But they didn't appear ready to turn over any more big things to me. Why couldn't I contract with a new vendor without asking Dad's opinion? Why didn't they let me make decisions about opening and closing times? Hadn't I proven anything?

Dad's stubborn Sicilian streak made me want to quit some days. I didn't enjoy feeling like a basic employee on the occasions I questioned the status quo.

"We better unlock the front door before the hordes beat it down."

Vanessa laughed. "I'll do it. Don't forget to turn out those lights. Your dad'll have a fit."

"Haha. Hey, Vanessa?"

"Hmm?" She stopped and turned to face me, a gentle smile playing on her red-lipsticked mouth.

"Thanks. For everything. You know, like every day. Being here."

"Absolutely. I love it here. I love you. You're a wonderful woman, don't forget that."

I nodded, then turned back to the chapel room to turn off the chandeliers. Hearing her love for me brought unexpected tears. That's when Colin rubbed up against my ankle, bringing back the cheerful smile I woke up with that morning.

Brian and I had left some boxes on the floor in the stockroom, so I lifted them to the table. They'd be ready for Dad to unpack. I needed that stuff for the two trees we set up yesterday. I'd tell Dad as soon as he arrived. Whenever that might be.

I flounced with toddler-like anger into my office and closed the door since there were no customers in the store yet. I skimmed my computer calendar to find that late delivery date — Tuesday. Perfect.

I can't meet for dinner on Tuesday, but the rest is open.

My text whooshed to Brian. He had meetings all day, I recalled, so his quick response surprised me.

Wednesday? I'll find somewhere different to eat. Okay? Can't wait.

And I meant it. The door chime rang, so I left the office to help Vanessa on the floor. Between customers and decorating two Christmas trees, we had enough to do. I must ask her what project we should give Brittany, the high school kid who came in three days a week. She'd be here at three, so maybe I could sneak out a half hour early—just because.

Who was I kidding?

Sylvie's bridal shower day arrived with a golden sun burning in an azure November sky. The warm, crisp air crisp perfect for a hike, or anything outdoors. Brian said he'd missed me on his recent hike, so I agreed to a second one right before Thanksgiving. I expected all heck would break loose at the store, though all sorts of retail mayhem might happen well before the family sat down for turkey.

Disappointed we'd be spending the afternoon indoors at the country club, I asked the event manager if we could open a few doors onto the patio. The long corners of the white linen tablecloths fluttered when any light breeze snuck in. I inhaled deeply and stretched after I finished placing the Christmas-y centerpieces and the holiday-themed place cards I'd designed. Sylvie wanted a Christmas wedding. She'd get a bridal shower to match!

I'd been lucky to find a deep gold shantung sheath that stopped at the center of my knees. Youthful but tasteful enough to make all the country-club mommas happy. I wore ruby-inspired costume jewelry: a heavy necklace and matching chandelier earrings. I thought it could be too much, but Dad exclaimed loudly when I entered the den to model. He wasn't even distracted by the football game on TV. I guess I looked pretty nice.

I stumbled over to the gift table, wincing as my right foot tilted outward. My shoes were way too high, the stiletto heels giving no support. I sported flats every day at work, sometimes even lace-up sneakers completed my work uniform. I had not been thinking at all when these shoes called my name and said Angie, we'll go perfectly with your dress. Come. Come hither, indeed.

I puffed out a loud sigh. Perfect for the dress, but not for the girl wearing the darn things. Every girl's a sucker for a gorgeous pair of red shoes. All you gotta to do is ask Dorothy.

Mrs. Bradley arrived in a red-and-gold swirly printed dress that clung to her curves. When she saw the cardboard "Bridal Shower" sign I'd hung flutter upwards, she marched over to the open doors and shut them firmly. Any harder and there'd have been a slamming sound. Oh well, I just can't do this right either. I managed a sweet smile in her direction and continued to fiddle with the red roses on the gift table.

Sylvie and Constance Miller turned up shortly after their momma. Distracted by all the decorating I had to do, I'd forgotten that Sylvie's sister had promised to help me set up. *Thanks for nothing,* I thought wickedly.

My dearest friend offered me an excited squeal as I wobbled toward her, her arms stretched out in front like Frankenstein, waiting for a hug. I held onto her for dear life. I'd missed her so.

"Oh, Ang, everything looks gorgeous! And like Christmas! You're amazing. Thank you for hosting."

"Apparently, it's what a friend's gotta do to catch a glimpse of her absentee friend now and then." I poked my bottom lip out in a childish pout.

"Aww. You're silly." She glanced around the room again, then fixed her gaze on me. "I know it's true, really I do. I'm so sorry that moving to Richmond has made me practically disappear."

"I just miss you, Sylvie. Maybe we can do better after you're married?"

Sylvie grinned and nodded. "I promise! Actually, I'll have more time to travel home."

"How's that? What's going on?"

She leaned over casually to sniff the roses on the bride's table. Was she really making me wait for some big revelation?

"Big news, Sylvie?"

"Well, Pete and I've been talking, and his house needs attention. The yard is a nightmare. I'm gonna work on that for a while."

"You're quitting your job? Does Patrick know yet?"

"Pfft on Patrick. I'll resign when it suits me, but..."

I raised my eyebrows, waiting.

"I'll tender my resignation after our honeymoon, and work through February or so. Spring'll be a perfect time to start fiddling with plants."

"Wow. This is kinda huge news." I scratched the side of my nose, wondering how I'm supposed to react to this revelation. I can't imagine Sylvie not doing her strategic planning with businesses. It sounded kind of boring for her to become suddenly domesticated, but I wasn't about to say that. I needed to process the idea, not that it's actually my business.

"Of course, we'd also like to start a family."

I started to speak, but Sylvie squealed when the very blonde Claudine entered the small room we occupied. She had been one of Sylvie's high school majorette friends. While I'd been busy with my school clubs, Sylvie had practiced each summer and the fall terms in the marching band twirling a baton. Even so, none of that had interfered with our deep bond.

The catering manager, Katrina, pulled me aside to check on the head count again. I lifted my phone to check the time and understood her concern. Two o'clock was minutes away and only half the guests had arrived, most of them already obediently seated where a berry-trimmed placecard told them to.

I honestly hate tardiness, but this party was slipping out of my inexperienced, possibly inept, hands. A few feet away, Mrs. Bradley directed Constance Miller to switch a few placecards around. This was my event, and irritation bubbled up.

"Hey," Sylvie whispered, "ignore Momma."

I took a deep, anxiety-cleansing breath, and nodded. "Thanks for saving me from myself."

She chuckled as she pulled me against her side. How can I describe the glorious feeling of her arm around my shoulder?

"How many are missing?"

"Only about half so far. Surprised?"

"Nope. It's Birmingham. Thirty total, right?"

"Yep. What do you want to do? It's your party."

"It's ours." Sylvie squeezed me again and my heart melted a little, much like the butter pats on the table. I wished I'd bought fancy fans for the table setting. Who knew November would feel like early summer?

"Let's give 'em a few more. How about I bang a fork on a glass at two-fifteen? Most everyone should be here by then."

"Perfect. Let's go stand near the French doors and get the latecomers seated asap." Sylvie pointed to the entry way where an easel held a whiteboard announcing the "Sylvie Bradley Bridal Shower" in someone's gorgeous loopy cursive. I wished I could write like that. I shook my head. I don't know why I'm doing this lately. My writing's just fine. Just fine, period.

Chapter 11

Brian

I FOUND MYSELF ON a serious romantic high with the progress I was making with Angie.

Would she say I was rushing things when I asked to introduce her to my family? We'd been dating for at least six weeks. Thanksgiving fell on the upcoming Thursday and I was considering the wisdom of asking Angie. She'd probably say no, beg off for family time or something. It's been a busy time for her. I'd be understanding, but disappointed as all get out.

I'd already shut down my Flirtable account. Heck, I shut that down the day after Angie agreed to go hiking the first time. I couldn't be distracted if I was to treat Angie the way she deserved.

I woke that morning with a full heart and a big smile. Every time we've been together, I learned so much and felt certain Angie wanted to spend more time with me. She'd gone out of her way, no matter how busy, to give this relationship the time any new couple needs. Are we a couple? It seemed that way to me, but what did she think about us and a future?

We'd be joining my group's Sunday hike again. I couldn't say for sure that she'd fully embraced the activity, but she had gamely strutted her stuff through the woods, over roots and rocky streams.

Perhaps I would try some special signal that I don't want our space invaded on the trail. That'd be rude, right? My parents taught me better. Hikers are the best people, and they expect to be treated well by everyone on the trails. I'd have to figure something out.

Heading to Ruffner Mountain again meant I picked her up in the same parking lot as our first hike.

"So, we're going on the same trail?" Angie asked as we pulled into the lot near the pavilion.

"Several trail heads start here. We're combining the Overlook Trail with another one. It'll be about three miles out and back."

"Three miles out?" She looked at me incredulously. I could almost see the wheels turning as she considered a longer hike.

I chuckled. "No, that's total."

"Well, I can surely do that." She gave me a grin as she punched my arm. Her bare hands already looked extra pink.

"Where're your gloves?"

"Shoot, in your truck. I'll—"

"I got 'em. Stay here."

While I walked back to the truck, Angie didn't stay, but walked toward the gang of hikers standing in a circle. Mike was talking, foggy breath forming a white wisp above his head. I trotted over behind her and rested my forearms on Angie's shoulders. The black gloves dangled in front of her and she snatched them with a giggle. As I leaned forward, she turned her head to the side, allowing my lips to brush her cheek. My stomach clenched with excitement, my face warmed by the surprise of that sweet gesture between us. An accidental kiss! I studied her profile, wondering what was going through her mind.

Across the circle, Kayla watched us, a frown playing around her eyes. Awfully curious behavior, considering she'd recently begun dating Grant from the group. Or so

I heard. Hiker gossip can be as unreliable as that of a high school clique. He was notably absent that day.

The group of twenty set out in small bunches, a thick line weaving into the woods. Angie had bravely volunteered us to sweep, assuring me that she also wanted me to herself.

"Tell me about the bridal shower."

"I thought I told you on the phone the other night," she asserted as she squinted at me.

"You did. But that was a pretty short phone call. I bet there's more to tell."

Angie sighed. "I probably shouldn't be telling you this, but Sylvie's momma might have been disappointed."

"What? After all that work you did?"

"Well... she's a funny bird. She did a couple of things that made me believe I'd failed on some level."

"What about the bride? Doesn't she count most?"

"She loved it. I mean, truly loved it. I thought everything was beautiful and so did she."

"That's all that matters then."

"Final word, huh?" She giggled.

"Final," I replied as I put my arm around her shoulder. We walked that way for a few minutes until we had to step over a fallen tree. The tree was too big for the group to move it, as we usually did.

"Sylvie's wedding is only four weeks away. December twenty-second."

"Do you have more wedding projects?"

"No, not really. One more dress fitting. And the hair and nails stuff."

"Right. I remember that from my brothers' weddings."

"You got your nails done?" Angie gave me a silly grin.

"Funny girl."

"Um... can I ask you something?" Angie looked down at the ground, avoiding my gaze. We wove around rocks and roots while she formed her question. I wasn't sure what to expect.

"Ask me anything. Wait... is it personal?"

She shook her head and remained silent.

"Okay, I know it's a ways out, and I may be assuming things and..." At that moment, Angie tripped over a root and tumbled with arms waving.

"Ahh," she squawked as she propelled forward, not so gracefully. Amazingly, she maintained her balance and didn't go sprawling on the dirt and dead leaves. I came up beside her to steady her. She brushed her hair out of her eyes and adjusted her jacket hood on her head.

"Angie! You okay? That was a pretty awesome dance to stay upright!" The dappled sunlight caught gold glints in her eyes and dazzled me. Suddenly, a similar unsteadiness struck my body. I pulled her into a hug, which she returned by wrapping her arms around my waist. We stood like that, completely unaware that the group had stopped until I saw them turn and move as one into the gnarled, leafless trees ahead.

Angie leaned against me, quiet. Her slow, steady breathing offered evidence that she was okay.

"You still have a question for me?"

"Would you be my wedding date?" Doubt and worry clouded her face, as if I would turn down a chance to spend time with her.

"I thought you'd never ask."

Forehead to forehead, we chuckled, then headed down the trail after the group. We quickened our pace until we were in sight of the group. We were responsible as the sweeps, after all.

"Tell me about the happy couple, then."

Angie shared the story of Pete and Sylvie meeting and the call she got when Pete proposed mere months later.

"Oh my gosh," Angie said as she described seeing a photo of Sylvie's hand. Her left hand. With a ring on it.

It sparkled with life and their love even in a simple hand photo.

"Pete finally put a ring on it," she chuckled. "And I bounced around my office and danced, shaking my booty. Oops, I probably shouldn't have shared that part."

"Hey," I responded, nudging her with my elbow. "Guys love a good visual."

Pete had taken Sylvie to the campus of the University of Virginia, so she could see where he'd studied literature. After becoming a famous — make that very famous — author, one of the library study rooms had a nameplate in his honor. He walked her over to The Rotunda, which was modeled after The Parthenon in Rome—Angie's telling filled in all the details—where on the wide steps he got down on one knee and asked her to marry him. Then he asked a student passing by to take their photo with the fancy camera he'd brought along as a prop, because Sylvie had believed capturing nature photos was the purpose of the entire day.

"I swooned while she told the story. I loved how he had tricked her, making me like him all the more. He didn't waste any time either, since they'd only met last November. It took 'em till New Year's Day to proclaim the feelings they'd been fighting for weeks."

"They'd been fighting for weeks?" I asked, already worried about the marriage.

"Fighting their feelings, I meant. It's a long story. We'll get to all of it, I'm sure."

"Okay, get back to the story. Is there more?" Of course, Angie had more to tell.

Apparently, Pete gave a lot of credit to Angie for the entire relationship.

"Pete thanked me for my enthusiasm. Said I sounded as excited as them. And he thanked me again for everything I did to keep them together."

"That's quite a romantic tale, Angie."

"Meant to be, as the country song goes."

Angie had asked them if they would have a long or short engagement.

"Short," they'd said in unison over Pete's car speaker-phone.

"Then Sylvie said, 'about that short engagement. My mom'll be calling you. We're gonna have the wedding in Birmingham, of course. As my maid of honor, you'll be helping. A lot probably, since I'm so far away.'"

The couple had decided on July, giving Angie and Sylvie's family only five months to pull it together.

Of course, the July wedding idea fizzled like an old firework. Pete's screenplay project got in the way, and so did the sad difficulty of finding the best-wedding-dress-ever in only a few months. They both loved Christmas most of all, and that became the next best option. Busy time of year for Angie, but as she ended the story, she said, "I'll do almost anything for my best friend."

"So, how are they doing these days?"

"Good." Creases wrinkle her forehead. "Why'd you ask?"

"Well... engagements can be tough on a couple. You've experienced the stress of a shower. Imagine the stress of an entire wedding."

"You sound like you know something about that. Your brothers?"

"Um, well, I was engaged once."

Angie stopped on the trail, bending down to tie a shoelace. I turned my back on our hiking group and watched her, nervous about what was coming next. Learning about and seeing firsthand her deep-seated general anxiety had been difficult, and I assumed that in our future there would be lessons I'd gain, mistakes I'd make.

When she stood, her bottom lashes were wet. Why was she crying? Oh boy, what had I done?

"So. When were you engaged?" Angie stared over my shoulder. Given her expression, I assumed a bear might be headed my way, but I wasn't about to take my eyes off her, even if it saved my life.

"We — um, Jeanette and I — got engaged our senior year."

"In high school?" She was squinting at me again. The idea of a high school engagement, considering what a doofus I was back then—maybe I still was—well, what a funny idea. But no way would I laugh in her face.

I shook my head. "No, last semester of college. Or like at Christmas, I mean. And we planned to have a wedding that summer after graduation."

I took a few steps toward her, slowly, since she seemed skittish as a kitten in a new home. Her shoulders slumped, but she kept her eyes on me. Her silence screamed like an accusation. I needed to fix this, whatever this problem might be. I'm not engaged now—and Angie's the one I was pursuing. What's the problem, I wanted to ask, but no way was I beating a hornet's nest. I could practically see the threatening flying beasts approaching.

"Uh, I'm not sure what else to say. Should I have told you before? I'm confused, I guess."

"Let's walk and talk, okay? Our group disappeared again." Angie swiveled around and took off.

"Right." I stretched my stride to catch up with her, leaves crunching under our shoes. I stammered, "Angie, I'm sorry. I screwed up."

"No," Angie said firmly. "You did not screw up. It's me, just stupid me."

"Surprised, sure. Stupid is not a word I'd ever use to describe you."

She glanced sideways at me, so I smiled.

"Tell me about her."

"Uh, really? Okay. Um..." I studied her profile, eyes intent on the trail's rocks and sticks that can take the steadiest hiker down if they're not paying attention. She's so pretty, with the sweetest youthful features—like the girl-next-door. She bit her lip and looked over, catching me staring at her.

I smiled again. I'm wondered if a kiss would make things better, brush away whatever doubts she had about me after learning I'd been engaged before. I didn't understand what the big deal was — such a long ago piece of my past. But kissing her, yeah, I wanted to do that. Based on her tortured expression, I ditched the idea of finding mistletoe in the woods.

"If you don't want to—"

"I will, sorry. I was searching for a new way to say how pretty you are."

"Changing the subject?"

"Sharing a truth." I shrugged and zipped my jacket up a little higher. The breeze had picked up just as the sun slid behind a cloud. "I'll tell you about Jeanette."

"Wait. This isn't the engineering major you studied with, is it?"

"That was Maggie."

Angie snorted. I knew what she was thinking—me and all my women. Haha.

So, I told her about falling for Jeanette my senior year and proposing after only a few months of dating. Christmas being such a good time for romantic gestures and all. Angie kept her head down and focused forward, seemingly avoiding my eyes while I spoke of loving another woman.

After graduation, she returned home to prepare for our life together—or so I expected—but the August wedding plans ground to a halt. Suddenly, Jeanette's calls and texts from Kansas grew further apart, and our hearts did too.

"I flew out there unannounced in July and she said she didn't really love me, and it was over."

"I'm so sorry. That must have been hard to hear."

"I begged her for more time, and suggested moving in together first. Her family would have no part of that, she assured me. So I left with my tail between my legs."

"Heartbroken?"

"Sure, but I took the lessons about trusting my feelings and women. And... I'm still single." I chuckled ruefully.

Angie stopped and turned to face me. "I have trust issues, too. I've never been engaged, but I met a guy in college who I had seriously hoped would propose—at Christmas." She smirked.

"Hey, have you had a serious relationship recently? Or in the past ten years?"

She shook her head, scuffing at the leaves that pooled on the trail.

"Been twelve years since the Jeanette debacle and I haven't had a relationship last longer than six months."

"Aren't we a pair?" Angie's eyes didn't sparkle like they had earlier.

"We could be," I said, letting the double meaning flutter in the breeze between us.

Chapter 12

Angie

WHENEVER I WATCH A romantic Christmas movie on television, I get so annoyed at the person who won't step off the ledge in faith, who fears becoming vulnerable to the risk of rejection by the person they love. Of course, as a viewer, I had more information than the main character and I'm not blind to each character's flaw.

And I have few doubts about how Brian feels about us. I've gotten a strong sense of the romantic notions he's working through. Still, I remained stuck to the ground by fear's fateful glue. I couldn't face his rejection. Perhaps part of my stupid plan was to sabotage myself. Why else would I wave my weird flag right in front of him when he told me he'd been engaged before?

What a gut punch. Why did hearing that affect me so horribly, one might ask? Not a clue. Why should part of his past, a woman from twelve years ago, matter to me? Again, no clue. All I could remember were the waves of cold running over me like I was standing in a lake in winter, frigid water lapping against my chest. Just stupid. That's me. Stupid to expect he'd never had a serious girl in his life.

I wondered if stopping to tie my shoe scared him a little. I'd done it suddenly, without warning or words. Had he wondered if I had something lethal in the laces? Haha, so silly. I read too many crime novels, perhaps.

When we caught up with the rest of the hiking gang, I slipped across the path and talked to Gayle, who'd gestured for me to join her. She'd been nice to me on my first hike, encouraging even, since I was so clearly hesitant about hiking. I had been way more nervous about Brian, but she didn't need to know that. For the rest of the hike, we ended up talking about Christmas preparations — a lady after my own heart who was champing at the bit to put up her tree even though hubby was resistant to decorating "too early" as the naysayers like to say. Sometimes I even call those poor folks "joy-killers."

Our ride back to the park-and-ride had been a quiet, strained journey. Brian didn't bother to keep the conversation going after I uttered a few single word responses. He probably considered me rude, but was too good-natured a person to press me. Getting back in my car, I turned the radio off so I could drive home in silent contemplation—sure that Brian would never speak to me again because I'd acted like a jerk. An immature, insecure jerk.

On my bed, my phone buzzed against my leg. My laundry was in the dryer, so I lounged in my room listening to Christmas music on my turntable—an old movie soundtrack I found at a record store a few blocks over from the mercantile. I picked up the phone and saw a text from Brian.

Enjoyed hiking with you today. You okay?

I rolled my eyes, happy he wasn't there to see my irritation. I'd throw the poor guy a bone, after how terribly I behaved.

You may make a nature buff of me yet!

He sent a thumbs-up emoji. Should I say something else?

Hey, about your brother and his teen crew. I'd like to talk more about that.

Another emoji. Praying hands? Hmm. I figured he meant it like a thanks.

My phone lit up and the black screen with Brian's name in white letters shimmered in my hand. I didn't want to talk. Gosh, I've gotten really grumpy this year. The only big change had been the dating. I stared up at the ceiling and answered.

"Hi, Brian." Hiding my feelings had become sport over the past few months and my pleasant tone hid the overwhelming unhappiness coursing through my life. Brian excepted actually. He really was a bright spot. I needed to dwell on that a bit more, I thought, as I stuck my tongue out at my reflection in the bureau mirror across the room. Grumpy Angie needed to take a hike. Like, literally. Granted, I had no confidence in hitting the trails alone.

"Angie. John hasn't stopped talking about the chapel room since you let him visit last week."

I bit my lower lip. I'd let Brian show the space to his brother, and I'd gotten a fascinating woodwork lesson, plus too much information about the problems encountered when renovating an older building. John sounded like he knew what he was talking about. Still, I hesitated to make any improvements without my parents' permission.

"Um, Brian, um, I do not own that building. My parents do. And I, uh—"

"Talk to them. It has so much potential."

"It's not that easy. I told you my situation." On several occasions, I'd shared deeply with Brian about my frustrations with running, or not running, the business the way I wanted.

"I hear ya. John's teen crew would be cheap labor, though. You'd never get a better deal."

I exhaled. Surely, it sounded like an annoyed sigh. Setting my phone on the bedspread, I pushed my arms above my head as though I could push against the ceiling.

"You've gone quiet again. Like earlier today. Are we okay?"

"I'm stretching."

"I'm making you anxious again. I'm so sorry. I suck at this."

I stared down at my phone, the black screen telling me nothing but the time. What did he mean by "this"? Should I ask? Could I be bold enough?

"Suck at what, Brian?"

"Being in a relationship. I mean, we are, aren't we?"

I grinned at the same mirror I'd just stuck my tongue out at.

"Yeah, guess we are. I mean, you are attending a wedding with me. I just haven't asked you to sign the gift card. LOL!"

He chuckled. I loved hearing him laugh. It's like a soft velour blanket I could slip under and snuggle. Pondering the warmth of his laugh reminded me that earlier in the day I'd imagined myself in a frigid lake. I'm losing it. I made a note in my head to call my therapist—it'd been a while since we talked. And I'm busier than, well, you know.

"Wait, about the gift card. Do you have a gift for Sylvie and Pete yet?"

"Not yet. I'm still thinking." I'd been chewing my nails over it, to be honest. We sell lots of wedding gifts at the mercantile, but I see that stuff all day long and it seems so ordinary, not special. This is for my bestest best-friend, so I can't give her and Pete just any old thing.

"What if, um, John made them something? He does this beautiful intarsia woodwork."

"Oh no, I couldn't ask him to do that. What's intarsia? It sounds familiar."

"It's sort of mosaic with wood. He makes gorgeous stuff. What about a lazy Susan for the center of a table? Something like that."

"I remember. I've seen intarsia at design shows. It's expensive, labor-intensive. The wedding is weeks away, so how could we commission something on such short notice?"

"He has some stuff set aside. He started going to summer festivals this year. Let me send you a couple of pictures."

The whoosh of my message app filled the room. I opened Brian's message. The items in the photos were incredible, so beautiful. I loved the originality of John's designs, drawing me closer to the idea of a wedding gift for my special friend.

"Wow, Brian. He is so talented. Let me think about the gift idea. Plus, I'm going to show these pictures to my dad."

"Really? John would die to be in a store."

"I can't promise anything, you know. I have so little say around here."

"I understand, Angie. I won't tell John. But can you promise you'll also talk to him about the chapel again?"

"Yes," I whined out my answer. Just thinking about mentioning store ideas has always felt like climbing a hill with weights on. My life was full enough already without adding complications... or arguments.

"Okay. That's all I can ask. Better sign off and find dinner. Night, Angie."

"Talk to you soon!"

"Wait! I forgot the main reason for calling. Don't suppose you'd like to drive to Tuscaloosa to meet my family on Thursday afternoon?"

"Oh wow. We have our family Thanksgiving at my aunt's in Chelsea. I guess she lives closer to you than I do."

"Hmm. I'm having a crazy idea."

I giggled. "Scary crazy?"

"Is tree decorating scary? I bought a fake tree last week, and it's still in the box in my living room. What if you left your aunt's and came over to help me decorate it? You are way more talented than I am. I've seen your work."

"Um, yeah, I guess I can do that."

"Not crazy about the idea, huh?"

"Oh. Sorry, that didn't come out right. Just logistics questions in my head. What time?"

"Why don't we talk or text this week and settle the details? I'm not sure about my family plans either."

"Sounds like a plan! Well, kinda." I grabbed my empty wineglass, ready to head downstairs for a refill.

"Yeah, it's a good plan. Talk soon, Angie. Enjoy the rest of your night."

"You too. Bye."

"Bye, Angie."

Slipping my phone into my jeans' pocket, I opened my bedroom door and headed downstairs. My stomach's gurgling began halfway down. Since Mom was cooking, I was glad to be home for dinner this beautiful fall Sunday.

"Hi dear. I moved your wet clothes to the dryer a bit ago." Mom sported a creamy linen apron embroidered with rust and gold leaves, which I'm sure you got from the store when I was a baby.

"Thanks! How can I help with dinner? What smells so good?"

"I'd love your help with the sauce. I've made spinach ravioli."

"Yum. Hope you're making my favorite sauce," I said as I side-hugged Mom.

"Arrabbiatta."

"Spicy, yeah! Okay, tell me what to do." Arrabbiatta sauce is like a marinara with chili peppers or flakes.

"Put on an apron, Angela. You must take care of your clothes."

Mom pulled a black cotton apron off the back of the pantry door. "Kiss the cook" along with a wooden spoon emblazoned the bib, and I chuckled as I tied a bow at my back.

I peeked inside the fridge to get a glimpse of the ravioli Mom had made and smiled.

"That's a lot. We having company?"

"No, dear. Your father wanted extra to take to lunch this week. Says you've been too busy to eat. You'll waste away." Mom swatted my bottom with a tea towel.

I laughed as I swayed away from her, which revived memories of my ten-year-old self snatching food before dinner and getting the same swats from Mom. Only now, Mom's once-dark hair was textured by white streaks. So sad to witness her aging, but happy to see how beautiful and lively she remained.

"He's right. It's nuts. Wish we could hire more help."

Mom sighed and shook her head.

"Just because my record is broken doesn't mean I'm wrong, Mom."

"Yeah, yeah," she muttered.

"Oh, before I get my fingers all garlicky, I gotta show you these pictures Brian sent me."

"I finally get to see this handsome devil?"

"Uh, no, Mom. His brother does beautiful woodwork." I leaned my back against the counter beside her. Our heads almost touched while I scrolled the photos. The zing of chili flakes and the warmth of seared tomatoes filled the kitchen.

"Wow. Lovely."

"His work is perfection."

"Show your father. He loves that kind of thing."

"I will. At dinner. Better get chopping."

Mom and I stood together at the counter until we had everything in the giant simmer pot that had seen us through hundreds, perhaps thousands, of pasta dinners. I set the dining room table while Mom sliced bread and coated it with garlic butter. After the "wasting away" remark, I might've gotten away with helping myself to a piece from the baking sheet. Instead, I sat in the den with my snoozing dad. A football game filled the room with cheers of the college crowd, red and blue uniformed players moving across the screen. Professional teams weren't half as interesting as college ones.

A snort pulled my eyes away from the flat-screen on the wall to look at Dad. "Guess I dozed off," he said with a chuckle.

"Mom sent me to tell you dinner's almost ready. Ravioli."

He rubbed his hands together. "Yes, a family favorite. Right, my girl?" He pushed his recliner up to its normal position, the mechanics squeaking.

I stood, hands on my hips. Taking a deep breath, I almost jumped into a store discussion, but paused as I watched Dad lumber out of the room, stiff and tired. Tears prickled.

"You coming, sweetheart?" Dad's voice broke into my morbid reverie about my parents' ages and the store. And me being alone. All alone one day.

I wiped a flat palm across my damp cheeks after he turned back toward the kitchen.

"Comin'."

Mom had plated the ravioli on her favorite oval, hand-painted platter. Golden all over, it featured grapes and pomegranates, stunning in rich tones made richer by faint brush strokes. Nonna Caruso had blessed Mom with it the year I was born, from her own family collection. We sold a line of Italian stoneware at the store, but none of it held a candle to the platter holding our delicious dinner.

"Patty, this looks amazing," Dad said as he inhaled. "Smells even better. Mmm."

"Angela helped with the sauce, didn't you, dear?" Mom passed the basket of bread to me, and I took two pieces, unbothered by my waistline.

"I did. And we forgot the wine." I stood up, waving my mom back in her seat.

I returned from the kitchen and poured everyone a glass before sitting down. I ate while Mom and Dad talked about goings-on with the neighbors. The scents of tomato and garlic warmed the room, and I hugged myself.

"Cold?" Dad peered over his loaded fork.

"What? Oh, no," I answered with a shrug. "Just happy, I guess. When are we going to decorate the house?"

Dad looked over at Mom with a smile, and I wondered what that gaze meant. Mom ran a finger around the top of her glass, the sun making the red wine appear like rubies.

"How about when we get home from Thanksgiving at your Aunt Martha's house?"

I shook my head. "Can't."

"Plans? You're not going to the store on your day off, I hope." Dad shook his head.

"Nope. Brian asked me over to decorate his place—"

"You're going to his apartment?" My mom's voice tainted with worry.

"Condo. And, yes. First time for everything, right?"

"That reminds me... show those photos to your father."

"Dad, you're not gonna believe this stuff Brian's brother is making." I handed him my cell phone. "Just swipe through the photos."

Dad stared at my phone, glasses perched on the end of his nose. A smile played on his lips.

"Nice woodworking," Dad said, as he handed the phone back to me and picked up his fork again.

"That's it? 'Nice'?" Incredulous, I dropped my fork onto my plate, its clatter startling them both.

Dad stared straight at me. "Angie, honey, what do you want from me?"

"I'd like more say in the business. Like stop treating me like a college coed with silly notions. I've been out of college for ten years. Ten years! I've given you everything, and the most I've gotten is the computer upgrade."

"You run the showroom." Dad looked from me to Mom, hoping she'd chime in with something helpful to his cause, perhaps.

"I manage the staff—limited staff—and keep the floor designed and stocked. I wouldn't say I 'run' it," I retorted.

"What's the difference? You're in charge."

I snorted out a sarcastic laugh.

"I'm in charge? No, Dad, *you* are in charge. Of all of it. I must run everything past you. Oh, except where to display plates and hang pictures. I'm in charge of that. Whoopee!"

Dad got distracted by movement across the table where Mom was stacking dishes. He handed over his plate. "I'll help," he offered.

"No, absolutely not. You need to finish this conversation."

"Your input would be appreciated," he pleaded while she shook her head.

"This is on you, Matteo. Entirely on you." Mom grunted as she lifted the stack of dishes. Silverware shifted and clattered, but nothing hit the floor. I watched my parents' exchange like a tennis match, back and forth until my gaze returned to my dad, focused on folding his napkin into a tiny triangle.

"Dad," I said, hating the begging tone of it. I tossed back the rest of my wine.

"Angie. I have been hearing you. I have."

"Hearing me?" I swiped my hair away from my face, tucking curls behind my right ear. "You mean ignoring me? That's what you've been doing."

"I'm trying to leave you with a... a business that's stable and profitable well into the future."

"How am I supposed to enjoy such profits when I'm working six or seven days a week? I didn't take a single vacation day last summer. When will I ever go away for a week, unworried about the wellbeing of the store in my absence? Never. Since I can't staff the store the way I want."

Dad sighed. He picked up the wine bottle and poured the rest into our two glasses. He cast a wishful glance into the kitchen where Mom was humming as she loaded the dishwasher. I'm glad she left us to it, even if it wasn't going well for me.

"You're not always practical."

I scoffed. "Practical?"

Dad stared into his wine glass. I was so angry I might've enjoyed a little wine-induced oblivion.

"What's the last impractical thing I did?"

"Honey, let's discuss this after Christmas. This isn't the time."

"It's never time with you," I exclaimed, pushing my chair back and stalking out of the room.

"Well done, dear." I heard my mom mutter. Dad har-rumphed.

Not so well-played by me either. Whatever would I tell Brian now?

I threw myself onto my bed and pulled out my phone again, comforted by the whoosh of a sent text.

Hey, can you talk?

Sure, Ang. I'll call in a sec.

I laid back on the bedspread, flat on my back, knees up. I'd studied the textured ceiling while I waited for Sylvie to call. She must be so busy with wedding stuff. My nose burned, and hot tears drifted into my hairline.

Chapter 13

Brian

I LOVE MY FAMILY. Really, I do. No sarcasm here.

But after five hours, my stomach was stuffed, and sleepiness tickled my eyeballs. When I started looking at my watch, my brothers pulled out their wise guy act: two married men who loved to subject me to annoyingly funny commentary. No one outside the family could understand the stupid references from our childhood — like our treehouse capers, favorite movie lines, and ex-girlfriend critiques. My parents witnessed too many private jokes, eternally bewildered by what their three boys were guffawing about at dinner decades ago. The brotherly punishment continued against me, the last single man.

"Brian must have a date," Nick sang some made up tune.

"On Thanksgiving? We haven't talked to Gran yet," Mom said, peering at me over the book she was reading to the grandkids, who were snuggled against her on the old family sofa. They needed to replace that ratty thing.

"Mom, I'm sorry. I didn't think about Gran calling today. Tell her... well, I love her, sorry to miss the chat. And I'm not going out anywhere. Angie's coming to my place—"

My brothers hooted and cat-whistled as though we were all teens. I waved the noise away. How did Mom stand us back then?

"She's gonna help me decorate for Christmas."

More hooting from the brothers; they surely drive their wives nuts with their childishness.

"Look who's getting domesticated," chimed Nick.

I rolled my eyes.

"Boys, boys," I said as I pulled my fleece jacket off the back of the sofa.

"I'd like to meet her," my mom said as she stood up. "John called her 'adorable.' Wasn't that it, son?"

"Yep, Mom, ol' Brian here's got him a live one. That's how it looks to me." He laughed as he picked up his son and turned him upside down, squeals and laughter filling the room.

"I'm out. Gonna stop in the garage to say 'bye' to Dad."

"Make sure he doesn't recruit you to be his assistant mechanic for the night," warned Nick.

"I got a hot date, remember?" I wiggled my fingers at the kids as I pulled the front door shut. I walked up to the two-car garage at the far end of the driveway, its lights blazing bright as a radio blasted classic country music.

"Dad."

My dad lifted his head out from under the hood, wiping his hands on an oily red rag. He smiled as he ran a hand over his chin.

"This car's gonna break me."

"Money broke?"

"Nah, just wearing me down. I can't give up," he whispered, shaking his gray-haired head. He stared down into the engine, brand new chrome parts glistening under the fluorescent rods high above.

"Dad, I'm headed out. Wanted to say goodbye. Thanks for the delicious turkey. You sure know how to fry one."

He chuckled and stuck a dirty hand out to shake mine. "Good boy. You're leaving early?"

"Angie, the girl I told you about, um, she's coming over to decorate."

"Have fun, son."

"Thanks. And Dad..."

He looked up with tired eyes, his hands resting on the front frame. "Yeah?"

"You'll get that done, I'm sure of it. Can't wait for you to take me for a ride in your grand old Corvette."

"Your lips to God's ears," he said with a grin.

I headed to my truck. Checking my watch again, I cringed. I was cutting it close and still needed to make a stop.

Texted Angie.

You still good for four o'clock?

I started the truck and put it in gear, hoping for an answer by the next stop sign. Three dots fluttered on the screen of my phone, which rested on my left thigh. Come on, come on.

Four-thirty? They're hard to escape!

Relieved, I sent a quick thumbs up and gunned my truck toward Chelsea. I had over an hour's drive, a shopping stop, and the extra thirty minutes that Angie had awarded me.

Angie texted me when she turned into my complex, so I ran downstairs to meet her outside. Two nights before, I'd had this stupid dream in which Angie arrived hours late because she'd been taking the elevator up and down and wandering around my building, knocking on doors. Dreams...weird, anxious dreams.

There she was, standing by her car, adjusting her coat and looking around the parking lot. What was she thinking? My stomach took a tumble as I realized she would soon be in my home, alone with me. Stuff of dreams, indeed. Without a coat, I shivered in the evening chill.

She ducked to peer into her side mirror, checking her lipstick or something. The evening light was getting a bit too dim for that to work, so I called out to her.

"Angie."

She stood quickly, startled.

Tucking my hands into my khakis' pockets, I moved toward her.

"Hey," she said as she gazed around. "This complex looks nice."

"Wait till you view my palace inside."

"Right here in Alabama."

We chuckled in unison.

I held open the door into the building's lobby, thankful that the small fake Christmas tree at the security desk was gaining life—multi-colored lights twinkled, adding extra richness to the plain silver balls that hung from the tree's tiny branches.

"Let's take the elevator," I waved my arm in the direction of the steel doors, suddenly worried about what we'd say in that confined space. Angie didn't look worried, a small smile playing on her lips, which shone with a rosy lip gloss. Seeing her so relaxed raised my curiosity about my nervousness. My feelings for her galloped around my head. My heart pounded so hard in my ears, I feared she could hear it. I looked down at my chest, hoping my heartbeat wasn't evident through my favorite polo shirt. I chuckled as I pressed the button to the third floor.

"Top floor, huh? You didn't tell me you had the penthouse."

"Pfft. Not even. I'd planned to say 'welcome to my humble abode' when I open my front door. It's a simple bachelor pad."

"I'll be the judge of that."

I raised an eyebrow in her direction. "Please don't get out the white gloves!"

"Are you kidding?" She snickered. "You've witnessed my crazy office."

"True. But that's a workspace, and totally different."

"You really are too nice, aren't you?" Angie turned toward me, looking up into my eyes. Totally kissable, but a ding sound erased the temptation. The doors opened into a carpeted hallway, home to eight doors for eight condos. I motioned for her to step out first. She hesitated on the carpet, not knowing which way to go.

"Oh, sorry, this way."

I led her to the last door on the right.

"End unit, nice."

"Yeah, wait till you see the views." I wiggled my eyebrows. She laughed, shaking her head.

"I'm nice and amusing, great," I muttered as I keyed in the lock code. Angie looked away while I punched in the numbers. I'm reminded of the romantic gesture of a door key in a gift box, a man or woman offering an important part of their life in the form of a bland item filled with enormous promise. The key code could be shared in a less remarkable fashion, and I flushed at the idea of giving this six-digit gift to Angie. The door beeped and flashed red, much like my cheeks, embarrassment taking over my brain.

"Dang it," I muttered, punching the code in again more forcefully. Angie was watching now with a wicked grin on her face. She had to know I was nervous as heck.

The door's rubber seal whispered across the wood floors as Angie walked in ahead of me, on high alert I could tell. So anxious to greet Angie, I'd forgotten to switch off the turntable. Soft tones of Sinatra singing about home for Christmas greeted us.

Angie spun around as she entered the living room, still wearing her black coat, and smiled. "Old blue eyes? You did pay attention to me."

"I bought it the other day at CJ's down the street from you."

"I can't get in there enough. I've been meaning to look for a Bing Crosby album missing from my Christmas collection, but... no time," she said as she shook her head and smirked. Time seemed a real theme for her, and I wished I could help. But how?

"So you approve of the music. Now, how about the decor?" I cringed that I'd asked it at all. Inviting an expert to comment suddenly made me sweat. "Never mind, don't say a word."

"Why? It's fine. You've got some nice artwork, and the leather sofa is amazing," she said as she ran a hand over the arm before sitting down on it. "Man, this is comfy. Nap time?"

Goose bumps rose on my arms. Was that an invitation? The silence grew embarrassingly long, with Angie clearly awaited a response.

I laughed.

"No nap for you, Angie, no matter how sleepy the turkey meal made you. You're here to work, remember? You owe me."

"Oh, I owe you now?"

I pointed to the seven-foot tree in front of my balcony window. I'd plugged it in to test the lights before she arrived. The white lights reflected in the sliding glass doors; the night was as black as the parking lot asphalt on the other side.

"Let's go," I cheered, clapping my hands and grinning. "What if we start by opening everything and see what I have?"

"You bought all this new this year?"

"Um, yeah. This is my first bachelor tree."

"Lucky me to get to help," Angie said as she opened bags emblazoned with two different craft store logos. "Wow, you got a lot of stuff." She turned around, taking in all the boxes at her feet.

"Too much?"

"If it's all for the tree, um, whatever. Let's get the tree done and decide what else we can do. That mantle over there is begging for some merriment."

That cream-painted mantle above my gas logs (which I may never use) needed attention, and I had no idea where to start. In answer to Angie, I nodded thoughtfully, like I understood how it would all go.

Hanging ornaments and chatting made the time fly by. We'd been at it for nearly an hour when I asked the big question about John's work.

"Angie. If I'm outta line, please say so, but did you mention John's woodwork to your dad? I recognize this is a bad time of year and all."

Murmurs and sniffles reached around the tree and yanked at my heartstrings. Stepping around to the other side, I found Angie staring through the balcony door. She wiped her cheek before turning back to me. "Sorry. I'm..."

"No, I'm the one to apologize. The store stuff has you stressed to the breaking point, and I'm adding to it."

She shook her head, her face puckering like she was about to cry more. With my arms open, she fell against me, a sob breaking free. I stroked her hair while she shook with emotion. Everything about her was so soft. I wanted to hold her like that forever. I wondered again how I could help her, me being "problem-solving Brian" and all.

She pulled away, lifting a corner of her long cardigan to dab under her eyes. "I'm a mess, so sorry. To answer your question—my dad liked John's work. But..." She took a deep breath and lifted her hands above her head.

"Gimme a minute?"

"Let's take a break and have some wine. White or red?"

"White, please."

I watched her stretch upward while I got glasses from my wet bar and the just-purchased wine from the fridge. Was it cold enough? Well, it would have to do.

Once we got settled on my sofa, Angie angled toward me and talked and talked, dabbing her eyes with an old handkerchief I found in a drawer. No tissues in the house—a problem I should fix. I got a fuller picture of her frustration with her parents and the store while I listened. Hard to do, given how much I wanted to help. She was so beautiful, and I hated to see her torturing herself.

"I behaved so badly on Sunday. I've avoided my dad as much as I could." She blew out a frustrated breath. "Today, with all the family, he just pretended nothing happened. That I hadn't exploded at him four days ago. I feel bad, really I do. But..."

"But?"

"Would your brother take orders for his woodwork? I especially like the cutting boards."

"I dunno. I think so. Let me text him."

"Wait." She laid a hand on mine, and a thrill pulsed through me. "Ask him about his turnaround time."

I went back to my phone, typing with two thumbs.

"Sent. What's this about, Angie? I thought your dad—"

"I'm making an executive decision." She stood. "Now, where's the potty?"

I chuckled and pointed to the hallway off the living room. While she was gone, I surveyed the Christmas tree debris. Organizing the boxes and empty bags wouldn't take long, so I launched myself into that project. By the time Angie returned to the living room, the tree was in full view from top to bottom. No boxes and bags littered its base.

"You don't have a tree skirt."

"A what?"

"Tree skirt. I'll get you one from the store. I have one in mind that'll go nicely with your snowflake topper."

I ran a hand over my head, confused by her Christmas decorating talk. "Okay. I think."

She waved me off and adjusted the garland that circled the tree. I watched her mess with the ornaments, allowing the warmth of the domesticated moment to flow over me. Her heavy sigh and the shift of her hands on her hips broke into my romantic reverie.

"What's wrong?" I looked at the tree glowing brightly with white lights and a random mess of ornaments. Maybe I'd overdone the store-bought crap, and it lacked something special. My eyes wandered around my place, trying to see it through a woman's eyes, and I became worried. What did these choices say about me? Was I sliding down the "good guy" column?

"I'll send you some pictures tomorrow from the store. We may have a few things you'd like."

"A few things? You're kidding, your store is awesome. Overwhelming, sure, but awesome. The overwhelming thing is just this ignorant guy talking. No offense, right?"

She nodded, eyes wandering around my place, then settling on the mantle. "There's a garland in the window." A finger tapped her lips. I let her do her thinking without me, given I'd be useless, anyway.

Her clap startled me. "K, what's next?"

Next? My brain scrambled for decorating ideas. I looked around, thinking about what to do.

Angie plopped onto the sofa and picked up her glass of wine. She sipped and stared at me over the rim. Okay, so "next" was just another activity. Still stumped, my hands began to sweat until I seized on an idea to keep her here longer.

"Movie?" My voice squeaked like a thirteen-year-old's.

"Do we have any popcorn?"

I stalled midway on my walk to the sofa and pivoted toward the kitchen. She had the good grace to follow me. While I dug around my pantry for the box of microwavable popcorn I was certain I had—*please let it not be expired*, I begged the universe—Angie poured more wine in both our glasses. Bless her. I needed it.

We settled in to watch a Christmas movie, but honestly, I didn't care what was on the big screen television across the room. Having Angie at my place, sitting side-by-side, was all I needed. Our feet propped up on my glass-topped coffee table, we struggled mightily to stay apart, until eventually, toes touched and stayed that way. She slipped her hand in mine. I studied her profile, but looked away when her face turned toward me.

"Oh gosh. What the—"

"Angie, what's wrong?"

"It's one o'clock. I gotta go."

I rubbed my eyes and looked up at the beautiful woman standing over me. Hands on her hips—again—she surveyed the floor.

"My shoes?"

"Um." I threw off the soft gray throw we'd snuggled under as the movie got under way. I saw her shoes under a bar stool near the kitchen. "Over there." I pointed.

She huffed across the room, then hopped to get her shoes on quickly. Still trying to wake up on the sofa, I wasn't much help.

"Angie, why don't you just stay? It's late, and it's a thirty-minute drive."

"No," she said it so definitively, the forcefulness struck me.

"I have a guest room."

She shook her head while she gathered her jacket and purse. The rattle of keys brought me off the sofa.

"I'll walk you out."

"I'm sorry I can't stay. We open at eight for Black Friday."

Dang. I forgot about her retail hours. I had the day off tomorrow and a round of golf scheduled with my brothers.

"Wait." I pulled her against me. Brushing her hair back, I leaned in for a kiss.

"Brian."

I opened my eyes to find her staring at me.

"I want to stay. Please know that."

"Good, but—"

"More than anything, I want to."

"Then do?"

"If not for the early open. Besides, I have no clothes."

I wiggled my eyebrows.

She placed her hands flat on my chest.

"Next time?"

"I promise." She leaned in, her lips pliant against mine. When her hands drifted into my hair, I pushed her against the wall. Her lips parted for me, and I took full advantage of her openness. Groans and moans convinced me she would relent. I whispered against her lips, "Stay."

"I gotta go. Next time, I promise."

I smiled, our lips almost touching. "I'll hold you to it."

"I like how you hold me," she whispered in my ear. "I gotta go, Brian."

Next thing I knew, her red taillights flickered away into the night. I drifted back to my condo alone.

Chapter 14

Angie

I'VE NEVER CHECKED THE statistics for rainy Black Fridays, but this grandest day for gift shopping was often slow for the small guys. Big businesses get all the attention, so we depend on "small business Saturday" after Thanksgiving. Our regulars knew the drill—come to us for the personal touch and special items one can't find anywhere else.

I woke filled with anxiety and crazy thoughts. I'd tiptoed into the house at zero dark thirty, thankful my parents weren't waiting up for me like my high school days. Back then, I'd vacillated between mortified and arrogant. I could be a total brat, which I'd demonstrated yet again five days ago. I wasn't over that argument, not by a mile.

Granted, being over thirty meant I didn't get the steely stares or stern lectures for staying out late. Given the relationship drought I'd experienced for the past few years, a late night lecture had a welcome ring to it. Over coffee, my parents offered no commentary and asked no questions about my late date. Breakfast was a little too quiet, to be honest, but I didn't give it much thought.

First to the store, I surprised Vanessa by having all the lights on, doors unlocked, holiday music playing. Customer ready, oh yeah. We settled in for a quiet day, though.

We were ready to help anyone who just had to grab a decoration or two.

At ten, I was hiding in my office, buried under the usual paperwork, and the door chime tinkled past my busy brain. Vanessa's voice rose in a friendly tone as she greeted someone familiar. A knock on my doorjamb made me jump. Brian's smiling face melted my heart.

"Hi."

"I brought doughnuts," he said, lifting a white and green box as evidence.

"Yum. Thank you."

I dug out napkins and small paper plates from a drawer and led him back to the closet-sized space that served as our break room.

"Sit."

"I don't want to keep you."

"It's fine. Vanessa and Bailey have it covered. Dad's not here yet."

What a ridiculous blabbermouth I was. I chattered like I had something to hide or something to say. Which was it? Embarrassed, I clammed up, letting silence pour into that room, not caring when the walls started closing in. I smiled at Brian, sympathy for him cinching my heart. He deserved my sympathy because I was such an anxious mess. I must totally confuse him, I mused as I took a bite of a doughnut.

"My brother... um, he'd love to be in your store. If you can work it out."

"Wait. You're not golfing today?"

"Rain killed that. And I'd rather be here helping you, anyway."

"Helping me?"

"Whatever you need. I'm here."

Oh wow. Free labor. Good labor, the kind Dad won't pay for. I've got to stop with the family-store bitterness and get to work, I reminded myself for the millionth time.

"Well, I reckon I should put you to work, then."

"I'm at your service. But first…"

I turned around in the open doorway, and he slid an arm around my waist. I'm sure my face registered surprise as I gazed up at him.

"We didn't kiss long enough last night. Or this morning, I mean," he said with a mischievous grin.

He stifled my laugh with a quick, soft kiss on my lips. My knees turned to butter, and all the air left my lungs. His kiss asked for nothing in return, not in that moment, at least. We've been together enough for me to decipher his long gazes—he wanted me.

"Brian—"

"Don't talk about it. Let's leave our feelings here. Something important to ponder."

I straightened, struggling to grasp the weight of his words. Brian was so nice, too perfect. I couldn't build him up into something that wouldn't be real down the road. Yet, there I was, "pondering" as he suggested. He had a power over me, I couldn't deny. I'd quit Flirtable, politely ended communication with Jake, and spent all my free moments thinking about this man.

"Shall we?" Brian touched my shoulder and pointed toward the stockroom.

I nodded, muted by the warmth of the kiss that lingered on my lips. We headed into the stockroom, empty of humans for now. Dad would meet Brian today, I guessed. Irrational fear knotted my stomach, but I took a deep breath and willed it away. I didn't doubt for a second that Dad and Brian would get along.

"I've been thinking that we should hide boxes of excess stock under the tables where it's displayed. Saves time during the rush."

"I'll start with a box-cutter; how does that sound?"

"Great. Can I leave you for a minute so I can check in with Vanessa?"

He gave me a salute and pulled a box off the shelving marked Christmas with black ink on a yellow index card taped to the edge.

I told Vanessa and Brittany about the doughnuts and explained what Brian and I would be doing on the floor. Vanessa agreed with my ideas. Brittany offered to check the drawers under the candle shelving to see if we had space for more stock. Gosh, to have a high schooler show initiative. I gave her a quick "you're the best" hug and hurried back to the stockroom.

Male voices reached me before I pushed open the stockroom door. Dad had already removed his jacket and was standing beside Brian, who was opening boxes.

"Met your fella here, Angela."

Obviously. I groaned inside, disappointed that I hadn't gotten the opportunity to control the meeting. Worry bubbled up. What a silly reaction. Deep breath, deep breath. Both men watched me, perhaps pondering my unsmiling silence.

Get over it, Ang, I told myself.

They were getting along, weren't they? Though only a few minutes in, I should be happy to accept Brian made a good first impression. I rubbed my hands down the sides of my black dress pants, deciding what to do. Or say.

"Yeah. Sorry, Dad, that ya'll haven't met yet, but—"

"Hon, I'm sure you appreciate the help." Dad winked at me, and I couldn't remember the last time he did that. What was going on? I habitually overthink things—anxiety does that—but accepting stuff at face value appeared to be my main task for this holiday season.

"Don't know if Brian told you what my plan is—"

"Do what you need. I've got a bunch of merchandise to return, so I'll leave you two be." He gave us a nod, and went to the corner where his desk was stacked on one side with small boxes and an old-fashioned Santa whose robe featured yellow, rather than white, fur trim. Pretty hideous, we'd all agreed last week when that late shipment had arrived.

Brian had no idea where the stock was displayed in the store, so he settled into the beast of burden role, carrying most of the boxes and putting them where I told him. We made a pretty good team, he agreed, but he waved off my suggestion that he leave his engineering job and work retail. Guess I hadn't sold him on all the rewards, I noted sarcastically.

"I hate that this place makes you cry sometimes," he said as he touched my shoulder lightly. That only made me want to cry more.

Before I could respond, my phone buzzed in my blazer pocket. Seeing it was Sylvie, I hit the "accept" button.

"Sylvie, happy Thanksgiving to you!"

"Oh, Angie, we've got a disaster on our hands."

"What's happened?"

"Haven't you heard the news? The Main caught on fire overnight, and it's... it's ruined!" Sylvie's sob flew across the miles.

"Hang on. Brian, look for news on the fire downtown."

He pulled out his phone and started typing. He held up a screen filled with links to the news story.

"Oh Sylvie. Do you think this means your venue is canceled?" I covered my eyes, thinking what a dumb question that was.

"No one is answering their phone. Momma has started on solutions already, calling the church and country club. What're we gonna do?"

"What does Pete say?"

"Calm as a stupid cucumber," she muttered with a bitter laugh.

I had the wisdom not to join in her laughter. This was a seriously serious problem, and she needed help.

"What do you want me to do? I'll do anything at all."

"Start thinking outside the box about places to have the ceremony. And the reception, oh my gosh, the catering. All up in smoke."

Literally, I wanted to add.

"Shouldn't you wait to talk to The Main's management? They may have some alternatives for you."

"Yeah, yeah," Sylvie's voice drifted off. She was whispering to someone. Pete, I guessed.

"Okay, listen. I'll give this some serious thought while I work today. Do you want me to run ideas by you before I call places?"

"I don't think so. Time is so tight. Twenty-five days, Ang. It's all we've got."

With my free hand, I straightened a tablecloth over the boxes Brian had just stashed. He watched me, clearly listening to my side of the conversation. I hoped he had a good idea or three.

"Sylvie, keep me in the loop about what your momma finds out, okay?"

"I will. I'm so sorry to call with this at your busy time. It's the last thing you need on your plate."

"Hey, bestie, it's okay. But start looking online too. If you want me to go visit some spot, take photos, you know, whatever. Just ask."

"K. Thanks, Angie. You're the best."

"Yeah, well, let's wait on that praise."

She clicked off, and I stood still, staring into space, thoughts racing. Brian had gone back for more boxes, so I headed in that direction. When his face appeared in the stockroom door window, I backed away to let him push through.

"That was intense. I take it that place is... was the wedding venue?"

"Yep. She hasn't talked to the management there yet. She's not waiting on them, and I have to start searching for a new venue."

"Geesh, that sucks. Big time. Where do these go?" Brian lifted the stack of boxes containing crystal angel ornaments.

"Oh, right. Hmm…" I scanned the Christmas trees that dotted the store. "I've no idea! No wait, over there." I gestured for Brian to follow me, lifting a tablecloth to allow him to slide the boxes underneath.

He stood with a grunt. "This is a lot of work. I can't believe you do this every day."

I raised an eyebrow at Brian. "It ain't engineering, but it takes a little thinking now and then."

"What next?"

"I need to brainstorm. Sylvie's problem is now mine. You don't happen to know of any places where we can hold a wedding, do you?"

He grimaced and shrugged his shoulders. "My brothers got married in Tuscaloosa."

"Okay, can you do something for me? For Sylvie and Pete, really."

"Name it."

"You search for caterers. Here's a notepad to write it all down. I'll search for venues."

"Won't we find some of same places? Venues that cater?"

"Well, we may duplicate some work, but that may be a good thing. Let's search first, then put it all together on a calling list. Make sense?"

"Yeah. What about the store?" He gestured behind him, as customer chatter reached us.

"Vanessa will come get me."

We got to work on opposite sides of my desk. Brian bent over his cellphone while I fed my laptop some magic words that I prayed would conjure a wedding venue. An hour later, we were startled by a tap on my open door. It was Dad, putting on his jacket.

"Headed out?"

"Not in the least. Wanted to see if you'd like pizza for lunch. Gonna run down the block to Gino's."

I looked at Brian, eyebrows raised. "Good for you?"

Brian nodded and turned toward my dad. "Thank you, sir. That's nice."

"Favorite toppings, young man?"

"I'm a pepperoni guy."

"Me too!" Dad exclaimed with amusement, like he was comparing notes with a newfound friend. At age ten, perhaps.

"Thanks, Dad," I said as I bent my head back to my notes.

"Thirty minutes. I've told Vanessa and Brittany..." Dad's voice drifted off when he saw I was too absorbed in my research.

"Gosh, I'm starved. How's your list coming?" Brian's voice broke through my troubled brain.

I sighed and ran my hand through my curls. "I dunno. Some places are so big, others are too small. Goldilocks revisited."

"Yeah. How big is the guest list?"

"Maybe like a hundred people? Sylvie's been away a long time, and Pete's from Virginia, so—"

"Come here," Brian said as he headed out of my office.

"Wait. What are—"

"Let's talk through something."

He grabbed my hand, walking so fast he practically dragged me to the stockroom. When he headed to the "chapel" space, I protested.

"No, no, no. This won't work, and my dad said—"

"Just hear me out."

The whoosh of heartbeats played to the tune of my negative thoughts. Brian was wasting time. And why was he so obsessed with this room? I didn't get it. And I told him so.

He ignored me and pointed to sections of the space, describing how a wedding could be staged. He strode the length of it, whispering numbers under his breath.

"You can probably fit a hundred-forty chairs. Seventy on each side of a narrow aisle."

"Brian, we... I... can't. It's impossible."

"Hard, but not impossible." He crossed his arms, turning in a wide circle, counting and measuring in his head.

"But there's no time, and... this can't work. Again, my dad would go nuts."

"Isn't he friends with the family? Maybe he'd like helping them out."

Gosh, this man infuriated me. Brian to the rescue. He relished the role, I could tell. I stood there just shaking my head.

"Why are you being so negative?"

"One, my dad already pooh-poohed doing anything in this space. Two, there's no option for food. Three, no dressing rooms. Four, little parking. Five, the bride comes in off the street — what if it's raining? Want me to go on?"

Brian pursed his lips after my brilliant take-down of his idea. Score one for Angie! I may come across as someone who's a little — okay, a lot — insecure, but I know a thing or two.

"I'll consider that," he said as he ran a hand over the rich, chocolate brown paneling.

I threw my hands up in the air and stormed out through the back hallway, grumbling about how stubborn Brian was. Dog with a bone, and all that.

Then I caught a whiff of hot tomato sauce and pizza dough. My stomach growled so hard I felt it rumble through my skin. Brian came up behind me, audibly sniffing and practically moaning.

"We're both starved. Let's eat and talk this through."

I growled at him, "Nothing to talk through. That room is off limits. I'm sorry. Will you help me with the venue list, please? After pizza?"

"Fine."

"What venue list?" My dad was plating pizza for himself.

"We have a disaster on our hands. I mean, I do, Sylvie does. Her venue had a major fire overnight."

"The Main? They were getting married there?" Dad frowned, apparently trying to picture a wedding there and coming up short.

I didn't love that venue, but it had some redeeming features. It was new and clean. Very chic, of course. Nothing less than I'd expect Sylvie to choose. And the contrast made our space all the more unappealing. Not that I was considering it, of course.

"Yes. And she suspects, but doesn't know for sure, that she's lost it for December twenty-second. Brian and I were researching alternatives I'm gonna call this afternoon."

"It's a holiday and you may get nowhere."

Thanks, Dad, for the vote of confidence. I didn't say it, just nodded while I chewed. Brian and Dad were already eating seconds. My hunger had dissipated after only one slice. All the stress of dating and the store problems really affected my appetite. I'd noticed the looseness of my pants that morning. I hoped my bridesmaid dress still fit. Dang it. I needed to schedule my final fitting! Overwhelmed took on fresh meaning.

As Dad predicted, Brian and I got nowhere with potential venues. Half of my calls went to voicemail and the other half were unavailable on that date. The invitations had gone out weeks ago, so a date change wasn't a viable option.

I lowered my forehead onto my desk, and fake cried. Brian chuckled and came around to stand behind me. His hands on my shoulders startled me, and then he began to press and knead my neck and back.

"Ohhh, that feels too good. Why are you so nice? I'm so mean to you sometimes."

"Shhh, relax. You're perfect."

No, I'm not, I wanted to say, but absorbed the words of a man who was making me feel oh-so-good.

Chapter 15

Brian

"Isn't this cozy? Angela?" A throaty voice clucked from the doorway. Angie jerked up like she'd been hit with high voltage.

"Mrs. Bradley, uh, oh. Um…"

I'd been standing behind Angie, massaging her shoulders and enjoying her low moans of relaxation. Angie's head rested on several legal pads of notes, and the organization of her brain came into focus for me as I surveyed her desk. She's smart, not erratic at all.

Her shoulders bucked when we were interrupted, and I pulled away. The proverbial cat got Angie's tongue, so I had to step in.

"I'm Brian, ma'am," I said as I walked around Angie's desk with hand outstretched. "You must be the bride's mother. Heard a lot about you."

The tall blonde woman in front of me raised an eyebrow, looking past me at Angie. "Charming boy, my dear. Good going." She chuckled, its tone rich with old southern charm.

"He's been helping me with the venue search," Angie blurted out, nervous as a cat in a room full of rocking chairs.

"So I see."

I had to chuckle at that one. Guiltily, I took a peek at Angie to see how she was doing. Taking deep breaths. I was on my own.

"Mrs. Uh…"

"Bradley," Angie chimed in.

Thinking she was taking over the explanation, I stood quietly in front of Mrs. Bradley, like a toy soldier. I looked over my shoulder as the silence lengthened. Wrong again. Angie was just sitting there, smiling.

"Mrs. Bradley, I am so sorry that your family has this… uh… disaster to deal with. We've spent—"

"I stopped by to tell Angie that I've failed to secure either the church or the club. I need more ideas."

"Okay, well… we've called almost two dozen places today. Left voicemails and crossed off other venues. So far, it's a bust. But I'm not giving up. I'll follow up on the unanswered calls on Monday. Someone's bound to call tomorrow." Angie smiled at her friend's mom, brimming with sudden confidence, which was kinda surprising. I had very little understanding of this woman I was dating, that's for sure.

"You're such a dear friend of our Sylvie. If I have any inspiration of my own, I'll let you know right away. I'm just so overwhelmed, I can barely… do… anything."

That was quite a speech. The only thing she didn't do was put the back of her hand against her forehead. Eye roll time. Southern women were a special breed.

That genteel southern lady swirled away from the doorway and her tall navy-blue-suited figure disappeared, leaving a cloud of sweet perfume and overwhelming duties in her wake. Poor Angie. She had her head buried in her hands when I turned around.

"Hey. You okay?"

"No. I don't need this."

"You don't. You're right. You should talk to the bride about this."

"No, no, no. I can't let her down."

"Who's paying for this shindig?"

She shot me a dirty look. I was right, but she couldn't admit it. She picked up her phone to check the time.

"It's almost closing time, thank goodness. I'm done."

"Let me take you to dinner."

"No way. If anyone deserves to be taken to dinner, it is you. My gosh, you got more than you bargained for today."

I held up my hands. "I volunteered. My pleasure, Angie. Please go to dinner with me. I won't keep you out all night. Promise."

"Okay. Let me check in with everyone. Stay here a minute?"

After she left me in the office, I leaned back in the chair, staring at the ceiling. I couldn't get my mind off that chapel space. It was mesmerizing. So uniquely outfitted with the wood paneling and stained glass. I wanted to learn more about it, even if Angie's family didn't want to use the space for business. In college, I took a class about architecture, debating if that was the engineering field I preferred. Though I settled on civil engineering, I never forgot the beautiful photos showing the intricate details of the ancient buildings we studied. Buildings that lasted far longer than the people who designed or built them.

Angie stayed gone so long, I went out into the store to search, and where did I find her? On a stepstool, trying to straighten a star on the top of a tree.

"Good grief, Angie, why are you doing that?"

Angie grunted and handed the star to me. "A customer bought the topper on this tree. I had to find a replacement."

Stopping on the lower step of the stool, she looked me straight in the eye. Our proximity tempted me to lean in, and as she leaned toward me, I heard a throat clear. Angie's dad, the perfect moment-spoiler. It felt a little too much like an old movie.

"Ang. I'm headed home. Your mom has made open-faced hot turkey sandwiches."

"Oh, yum. But, uh..."

She looked at me, then back at her dad. "Brian's taking me to dinner."

That she saw it my way made me smile.

"Don't keep her out too late, young man." He grinned at us both.

"Right, Mr. Caruso. Early night, I promise."

He studied us for what felt like a minute too long, making me want to laugh. I ran a hand over my face to hide the temptation.

"Don't forget to lock up," he said over his shoulder. We watched him retreat into the stockroom, his red plaid shirt still visible through the door window.

Angie hopped down off the last step, the movement reminding me I'd wanted to kiss her a few minutes ago. She shook her head.

"Who is that person I want to stay mad at?"

I shook my head and wisely kept my mouth shut, knowing I didn't need to express an opinion about family matters.

"Isn't it closing time?" I asked, nodding at the short line of people waiting to check out.

"Shoot! I'll be right back. Uh... I hate to ask more of you, but would you mind dealing with the empty boxes we left on the worktable back there?" She nodded toward the stockroom.

I headed that way. Unsure what "dealing with the boxes" meant, I looked around the massive space, which was at least half the size of the store itself. Near the door, I spotted a metal rack holding all sizes of cardboard boxes, flattened. I treated the boxes we'd emptied that morning the same way. While I cut seam-tape and flattened them, I thought about Angie's dad, who kinda reminded me of my own—the same gray hair, similar build, though my dad was taller by a few inches.

When he'd entered the stockroom from the rolling door that morning, I'd nearly jumped out of my skin. I figured that it was Angie's dad, not that she resembled him. Made me curious about her mom, whether Angie took after her. Did Mrs. Caruso have big brown eyes and dark wavy hair? Were her lips soft and full?

"Hey," Angie's voice startled me out of my stupid musings. "Where were you?"

Guilty? Did I look like my mind was up to no good? I shook my head to clear it.

"Uh, where was I? Um, nowhere. Wondering if the rain was gone." I stuck my hands in my pockets and attempted a generic facial expression.

She'd already lost interest in my thoughts and had her hand inside another case of ornaments on a shelf by the door.

"Dang, I missed these." She hung her head and sighed.

"Hey, tomorrow's another day. Famous movie line, and a good one for this very moment."

"Yeah. Store's closed, the girls are gone. We should get out of here. Can we walk up to the cafe on the corner? I don't want to drive around town looking for dinner."

"Sure. Traffic'll still be a bear later when we head home, most likely."

"Be sure to lock up." Angie imitated her dad while she turned the key in the store's main entrance.

I couldn't resist a chuckle. "Ya'll have some stuff to work out, for sure."

"Maybe we will, maybe we won't."

Walking beside her, I bumped against her to emphasize my point. "Come on, be positive. A new year is nearly here. Make a plan?"

"A plan?" She stopped, turning to stare at me. She shook her head. "I don't think you really get it."

"Fair enough. I do not get it. But I'm here to support you, okay?"

"You're definitely an encouraging person, but I have to sort this out my way. Whatever that is."

I took her hand and pulled gently to get her walking again.

"I'm hungry. You?"

"Starved. One slice of pizza doesn't last long."

"That was nice of your dad to buy everyone lunch. Does he do that often?"

"Not really. I can't remember the last time he did." She nudged against me. "We have your presence to thank."

"Me? Huh."

"Thank goodness this place isn't busy!"

Angie stood aside to allow me to open the café door, and I warmed with pleasure that she recognized this gentlemanly side of me.

We ate a quick dinner, and as I'd promised Mr. Caruso, Angie was in her car before seven.

Just before ten, Angie texted me.

Thank you, thank you. You were great today.

I'd fallen asleep on the sofa and the gentle buzz and chime surprised me out of my slumber. I couldn't find the words to express how much the time with her had meant to me. I returned a thumbs-up emoji and stared at my phone's colorful screen, thinking about Angie's problems with her dad. And the problem with the wedding. Geesh, she had a lot going on.

Unable to stop thinking about her, I asked Angie about hiking on Sunday. Three dots bounced on the screen, then disappeared.

Yawning, I headed to bed. My brothers had secured a replacement tee time for tomorrow, and if I was going to beat them, I needed some rest. I'm not used to standing on my feet for hours a day. I was already pulling the covers over me when my phone lit up again with a reply from Angie.

Rain check? I think I'll need Sunday to work on the wedding problem.

I understand. I'll check in with you this weekend, though. Okay?

The heart eyes emoji jangled on the screen. Aww, she really likes me.

Was that such a revelation, though? Hadn't I had plenty of signs that she enjoyed my company? Granted, she could be pushing me back into the friend zone, except she did almost kiss me today. Darn her dad.

I'm sure I fell asleep with a big grin on my face.

Chapter 16

Angie

How did we make it through Small Business Saturday? The door chime never stopped ringing. But we were still surprised when I reported our day's sales had jumped twenty percent over the same day last year.

True to his word, Brian called on Sunday to check on me. After he'd witnessed a quiet Black Friday, Brian was shocked by my description of the bizarrely busy scene on the floor that day, but not at all taken aback when I told him that I'd made zero headway on the wedding venue problem. He was a little quiet about that and I couldn't help but feel he was letting the unused space idea simmer in the silence. I'm not calling it "the chapel" like he does because I cannot claim any belief in that—it's not a realistic solution.

Does it intrigue me? Yes, and all the credit goes to Brian, whose enthusiasm about it weirds me out a little. Having something like that gorgeous space so near and it containing the possibilities only he can see scared me a little. Okay, it scared me a lot. I can't manage another space; not when my dad doesn't believe in what I already do. He never seems to be on my side.

But I can't think about any of that, not while helping, or trying to help, solve the wedding venue problem. Or should I rephrase, *the catastrophe.*

Sylvie was completely beside herself when she called me on Sunday afternoon after Brian's call. I was relieved that I'd spoken to him first as I wasn't sure how I'd have treated him given the mood Sylvie's tearful goodbye had left me in. The first week of December didn't get an auspicious start.

When a week went by after the fire, I still had nothing to show for it. Mrs. Bradley also left a voicemail with a dismal report, as I'd refused to answer the phone when I saw her number. Seventeen days until the wedding, and we had nothing. My phone belonged in the trash can. I hated its inability to bring any good news to what should be a very happy time. The upcoming wedding, that is.

"Making Christmas" for everyone else in Birmingham was the underlying theme of our jobs at the mercantile, which always takes away a bit of the season's fun for us. Even Vanessa shared the sentiment.

Don't get me wrong, I do love Christmas. The Day. That's my name for it, behind closed doors. For the past few years, I've spent that special afternoon in bed, reading. Getting over the exhaustion of the days leading up to The Day was no easy feat, and certainly not accomplished in one Christmas afternoon. But not having to "people" all day long was one of its best joys. Thankfully, my parents understood and rarely badgered me about going to visit family members—and I got the house all to myself for a few hours.

I wandered to the stockroom and found my dad sweeping the floor. "I wish Otis were back, so you didn't have to work such long hours, Dad."

He just shook his head and kept sweeping. I sighed and sat in his desk chair, wheeling it back and forth like I did when I was very young.

"What's on your mind, Ang?"

"I want to show you something." He rolled his eyes, as though I was starting another argument.

"No argument, just come here. Please?"

He quietly followed me down the hallway to the unused space.

"Ang," Dad said, all his strong negative opinions etched on the way he said my name.

"Please hear me out." I pulled over an old chair and gestured for him to sit.

"We're desperate here, Dad. I think we need to offer this space to the Bradleys."

"For the wedding," he snorted with disbelief.

"Just offer. I can't imagine it fits the theme."

"I doubt it's big enough."

Yay! He hadn't killed the idea completely.

"Um, it's a small-ish wedding. A hundred invited. Some may not come, right?"

"Pete could be an attraction."

"Yeah. The draw of fame."

"I dunno, Ang. Whatcha got—two weeks?"

"Seventeen days, to be exact. But two weeks has to be the deadline for my plan."

"You have one?"

"Well, Brian showed me a couple of things. And his brother could bring a team to polish the wood, get things beautiful. How do you clean stained glass?"

Dad shrugged and started strolling around the room. He ran his hands down the wood paneling that stopped at about his chin level. "This is nice."

"Did you have plans for this when you bought up the rest of the block?"

He shook his head, his back to me. I wondered what was going on in that head of his and then he told me.

"I can't see it, honey. Reception food, changing rooms for the bridal party, parking—"

"Parking across the street at the city park?"

"Permission to do that? Inspection or zoning issues. You thought about that, hon?"

I shook my head, absorbing his words. He was right about it being too overwhelming to accomplish, let alone in two weeks. But his being right didn't make me appreciate him any.

"The Bradleys will figure this out. Don't stress out too much. It is their problem, after all."

Dejected, I turned to go. He put his arm around my shoulders.

"Why couldn't we explore options for this space in the near future?"

"Angie."

"Dad, I already said my piece about how you treat me in this business. When—?"

"I'll retire in a few years. Be patient."

"You're not being fair to me. I'm not sure I want to be in limbo anymore."

"We need to get back to the customers," he said as he gestured toward the door.

Just like him to change the subject. And make it about the customer. Sigh. I knew this busy season wasn't the time to have a debate about the store, but I was so over it. When would he make the store's most important decisions about me? I wanted to ask.

"You check with Vanessa. I need a minute." I headed to the street doors with the stained glass above.

"Ang. Don't."

My back to him, I waved him off. Thoughts about the store, this space, and the wedding ping-ponged around my brain. I couldn't settle on a single idea. Dad was gone, told by the squeak of the stockroom door.

My phone buzzed in my red blazer pocket. Sylvie, desperate to get good news, had sent her daily text. As if I'd forget to work on this! But I could forgive my distraught friend, now that I'd experienced a speck of the emotional drain of wedding planning. There I was, thrust in the middle of "the catastrophe."

Any news?
How flexible are you about the venue?
What do you mean?
Um, like a place that's never been used for a wedding. Ever. No kitchen attached. But absolutely gorgeous, though it's not modern like The Main.
Pictures?
Not ready for prime time, my friend. Give me a couple of days?

Three dots wiggled on the screen for what seemed like forever. Pete, the novelist, has rubbed off on her.

But you're still looking, right?

A short one. I wondered if she'd deleted a bunch of words to spare my feelings. That would be just like her.

Yes, but please realize we've exhausted almost every option.
So Mom tells me. She's a wreck too.

Is everything else in order? What about food? What were you going to serve originally? I should've asked before, I guess.

The dots appeared again. A screenshot of a menu arrived.

Got it. Talk later?
Yeah. How's Brian?
Going fine so far.

Sylvie sent me a heart eyes emoji. I pursed my lips. At least it wasn't the one she'd been sending me every other day—the one with streaming tears.

Chin up. We'll figure this out.

She sent a fingers-crossed emoji. Such faith she has.

I sat in the chair I'd pulled out for Dad and texted Brian, apologizing for interrupting his workday. Then I jumped straight to business.

Can John come with his teens this Saturday? I want to get the chapel space cleaned up.
For the wedding? Really? Wow!
Just in case. Still looking for other options.
It's a safe play. What does the family say?

Sylvie asked for pics, but I didn't send any.
Parents?
Haven't told them. My dad said no. Surprise, surprise.
What do you want John to do this weekend?
Clean the wood paneling, floor, and the stained glass.
Can I call after work? Wanna get dinner?
Yes and maybe!

I had to laugh, even though turmoil swam through my veins. Just texting made me want to see him again. And again.

Brian sent a question mark and a laughing emoji.

Give me till closing to decide about dinner. My office looks like a bomb exploded.

A thumbs-up emoji arrived, and I pocketed my phone. My phone buzzed again with a message from Brian.

John says he'll be there at ten on Saturday morning.

I spun around the space again and headed into the hallway in search of more wedding solutions. A cold, stinky bathroom was my first discovery. I hadn't known it existed. Turning the taps resulted in gurgling and sputtering, then a splatter of rust-colored water. The toilet didn't flush either. The handle jiggled. The door needed signage. I began a project list on my phone.

Dad admitted that when he bought this extra property, he had no ideas for it. I once heard him say he was keeping out riff-raff or something. Basically, he wanted to control who our work neighbors would be, and so far, we had none.

I kept wandering down the hallway, getting colder by the minute. Cobwebs waved from the ceiling vents as I passed underneath. Before I reached the door at the far end, I opened a door on either side exposing two small storefronts, or so they appeared to me with their large glass windows and doors opening onto the street. One opened on the same street as our store, the other on the back street that faced the city's park. I wondered how they'd once functioned without an alleyway for trash; this was definitely an odd building. Without a coat, I got too cold to spend much time poking around in the spaces littered with cardboard and a few merchandise cases, so I headed to the last door.

As I pushed it open, I tried to remember what businesses had occupied this block long ago. I remembered the papered-over windows and "Closed" signs from my teenage walks along the city sidewalks. There'd been quite a revival down here in the city's older business area, but had Dad inadvertently prevented progress around our booming business?

The heavy steel door opened into what may have once been a kitchen, judging by the long metal tables and a single white-and-gray marbled rolling pin that looked a lot like my mom's. No ovens or burners in sight. I put my hands on my hips and surveyed the room in a slow spin, which I'd been doing a lot of lately. What did I know about buildings? What had Dad said about inspections?

I blew out a breath, the only sound in the room which was only about twenty feet square. It didn't look like a normal kitchen—gutted when the business closed down. Another door led into a dining space with tiny tables. I wondered if it might have been an ice cream shop or some other restaurant that didn't need ovens. The floor in both sections — front and back — were decked in black-and-white tiles. They seemed to be in pretty good shape. I ran a hand down a textured white wall.

I hurried up the hallway, desperate to get to my office to finish the project list. I stopped to look at the bathroom again; the walls would need a coat of paint. And what was that smell? Mildew? I wrinkled my nose and shut the door tightly, keeping the unpleasantness from ruining the hallway's ambiance, barren though it was. With a little imagination and mercantile product, I figured I could improve the look of the space.

The wet, dark smell of the bathroom filled my head again, and black thoughts slid in with it. "This is impossible," I whispered.

I slipped past everyone in the store and into my office, tossing my phone on the desk in exasperation. I had no idea what I was doing. Run a wedding venue? Was that my new dream? Host a single wedding in two weeks? I'd completely lost my mind.

After closing my door, I leaned against it, taking lung-filling breaths. I'm useless to Sylvie. What had I been thinking? I knew nothing about event planning, let alone managing the minutiae of a wedding. And how stupid could I be to believe the mercantile building was fit to handle a wedding at all?

I grabbed my black wool coat and scooted to the exit, avoiding eye contact with Vanessa. The door chimed in my wake as I rushed onto the sidewalk, cold air slapping my face. The cold—I needed someone to look at the heating system too. Who would pay for all the work? "Oh lord, there's absolutely no way," I sniffled.

Walking aimlessly, I found myself in front of the cafe Brian and I'd recently visited. I stepped inside, its warmth curling around me like a blanket and highlighting the painful frigidity of this weird Alabama cold snap. A young girl behind the counter greeted me, but I approached hesitantly, unsure what I needed to ask.

"Um, do you guys cater?"

"Cater? Like events?" She looked over her shoulder toward the gray door leading to the kitchen. "Let me get the manager."

I pulled up the picture Sylvie had sent. The menu was more upscale than anything this cafe served, but I mentally crossed my fingers. The door swung open, and a petite woman hurried through. She wiped her flour-coated hands on a beige apron. "Hi. You wanted to see me?"

"I asked about catering."

Pushing wisps of pale hair out of her eyes, she nodded. "Sure, we can cater. Don't do it often, though. What are you thinking?"

I sighed and stuffed my hands in the pockets of my coat. "A friend's wedding. December twenty-second."

"Whoa." She chuckled.

"It was scheduled at The Main, the one that caught fire?"

"Yikes, that's too bad. I heard about that."

"Finding a venue. We've had zero luck, which is worse than bad luck, I think."

"Okay, so I'd like to help you out. But—"

"It's insane, I know. My family owns the mercantile. I'm messing with the idea of using an empty space on our block."

"I love your store! See that tree? Half the ornaments are from you."

"I appreciate that. I was in here the other night with my boy... friend," I faltered on the word. Calling Brian that sounded so foreign.

"We should all support each other. My name's Lisa, by the way."

"Angie."

"Listen, I don't think I can cater an event like The Main would. It'd have to be much simpler. Really simple, know what I mean?"

"I get it. Um, let me send you the original menu and we can discuss options. And, I haven't run any of this by the bride and her mom yet. But you know... time and options are running out."

We sat at a table and talked through menu substitutions to recreate Sylvie's version of a dream reception. I left the cafe with a bag of sandwiches to feed everyone at the store, buoyed by the promise of something coming together. Maybe, kinda, sorta.

My defiance would come home to roost eventually, I could be certain. Still, my confidence had grown that morning.

Until I met the woman talking to Dad in the stockroom.

Chapter 17

Brian

Five o'clock rolled around and with no response from Angie, I kept working on a project instead of heading out. She promised to reach out, so she'd be in touch soon. Perhaps she got slammed with customers right before closing, I rationalized.

My complicated assignment distracted me for an hour, and disappointment flooded me again when I looked at my phone. No messages. I tapped a mechanical pencil on a notepad. What to do? Driving to the store wasn't an option, as she'd probably locked up already.

Not wanting to accuse her of forgetting about me, I tried an open tone. I mean, she's in her busiest season, and I'd just be in the way, an unwanted distraction.

Hey, what's the plan?

I stuck my head out my office door. The office suite was empty and dark. Instead of working more on the project, I grabbed my jacket and hit the stairs. After running down five flights, I hit the bar on the door. Cold air pressed against me, almost like it was pushing me back inside. I pulled up my coat collar and walked to the back lot. I never park close, even when it's this ridiculously cold.

Unsure of the evening's plan with Angie, I headed home. I could still meet her for dinner, if she wanted. Experiencing the icy darkness tempted me to cook a pizza and chill, though. Not that I didn't relish hanging out with the delightful Angie. Things were growing between us, and I'd been getting heavy vibes from her, too.

But why had she gone silent on me today? By eight o'clock, when she hadn't responded to my text, I worried. Had she gotten sick, hurt herself? Something going on with her dad, maybe? She'd agreed to me calling and going to dinner, so making a call seemed the only option left. My phone lay silent on the cushion beside me, making me hesitate to call.

She could've texted me to let me know what's going on. I got a bad feeling in the pit of my stomach. The beer I'd just finished soured. Worry overtook all reason, while I paced the floor in front of the tree. It's joyful sparkling mocked me. Sorry I'd turned it on when I got home, I jerked the plug from the wall. The rattle of ornaments around the bottom caused me to stop and watch for any falling.

Shaking my head, I hit the call button for Angie. It rang over and over, going to voicemail. I listened to her sweet voice, but tossed the phone to the sofa rather than leaving a message. Frustrated, I ran a hand through my hair and started my pacing again.

Something was off. Angie had been available to me, always answering texts and calls without delay, and constantly cheerful. She seemed a thousand miles away, and I didn't like it. Not at all.

"Come on, Angie," I muttered into the space around my tree. Lost and worried, I took a long hot shower, replaying in my mind all the things we'd talked about the last few days. Searching for a sign of things going bad, but I discovered nothing.

I waited for an hour to pass before calling Angie again. My knees buckled when she answered on the fourth ring.

"Oh, gosh, Angie, I've been worried."

Silence.

"Angie? What's wrong?"

A sniffle traveled across the phone line. I waited, biting a hangnail on my thumb.

"I can't believe you snuck behind my back!" She wailed.

"Behind your back? I don't...What're you—"

"A lady from city hall came by today. I was out and my dad..."

Someone from the city? I blew out a harsh breath, remembering what I'd done. How did she know I was involved?

"Angie, I'm sorry. Can you start from the beginning? What happened today?"

"Oh, I'm not getting into it with you. You started this mess. 'Angie, you should run a wedding venue. Angie, you can fix this place up.' Arggghhh!" She ended her mocking words with a growl.

"Okay, yes, I did call the city. But just to ask about the age of the building. I swear."

Angie's scoff was followed by a silence so long I thought she'd hung up on me. Until I heard the sniffles again, followed by her screaming into the phone.

"I now understand how stupid I am in your eyes. Typical! You're just like my dad!"

"My dearest Angie, there's absolutely nothing stupid about you."

"You have a strange way to show—"

"Wait. I'm confused. What did the city lady say to upset you so much?"

I heard Angie breathing and she let out a long, sigh-like groan. So relieved that she was still talking and hadn't ended this call, I got another beer out of the fridge. The pop of the can got her attention.

Angie blew out another deep breath and started the story that prompted her to give me the silent treatment all evening.

When Angie returned to the store, she overheard her dad disparage the room and the work that Angie had mentioned doing. She took the woman and her dad into the room and shared her ideas. It became clear to the city employee that Angie planned to preserve the space. The woman took lots of photos and returned to her office, insisting Angie complete a renovation application for approval.

Angie realized that someone had called asking about the history of the location, and then she assumed I was the culprit. Angie was understandably furious about what she called my meddling.

Wisdom whispered in my ear, and I followed its admonition to keep quiet. Until she dropped a bomb on me.

"Perhaps we should take a break."

"A break?" My voice broke on the word, the unfairness of it all.

"Sorry, not sorry. I need some space to think. I don't think I'm the right girl for you anyway. What you did. And the…"

"I don't think I did anything."

"You haven't been listening then. Your meddling has delayed this wedding project and I…" She growled so loud I pulled the phone away from my ear.

"Wait, tell me why you aren't right for me?" I'd do anything to keep her on the phone, like we're together. And I could talk her out of such a silly idea.

"Brian." She sighed, the frustration reaching through the phone.

"We're perfect together. I'm… I'm crazy about you!"

"No. Stop. I'm a klutz, an anxious mess. Not outdoorsy enough. Get the picture?"

"I don't really, no. No, I don't get it."

"I need a break. Just don't call me."

"K," I choked out. I hung my head down, my chin resting on my neck. I wouldn't hang up. She'd have to. The heavy silence forced me to look to see that she was still on the line.

"Angie?"

She sniffled. Through a sob, she said, "Gotta go."

And she was gone. Elbows resting on my thighs, I stared at the phone. Willing her to change her mind wouldn't work. How stubborn could she be? What was I thinking anyway, pot and kettle? My brothers have long accused me of stubbornness.

I started pacing again, searching for a solution to this problem I'd apparently caused. Then I remembered my brother and the work he's supposed to do in two days. My stomach clenched painfully. I wouldn't get in the way of Angie's project again.

Here's John's contact info.

My text remained unanswered until the morning.

Thx

Her skimpy reply told me this was for real.

I mistakenly poured a full cup of milk into my coffee cup instead of my favorite dark brew. My mind went numb while I lay in bed, becoming familiar with my ceiling and trying to convince myself that Angie would not carry out her threat of taking a break.

All my replays of the phone conversation revealed nothing new. With Angie beyond angry with me, my defenses were on high alert. I hadn't done anything wrong. Had I?

I needed to give her time to get over this... this over-reaction to my so-called meddling.

I'd left work late the night before with two projects in the review phase, so I could easily take off a day. It was Friday and less than three weeks from Christmas—my boss understood. I just didn't want to mope around my condo all day.

I texted John.

Hey, bro. Angie's gonna reach out to you directly. Easier without me in the middle.

And me out of her hair.

After John responded with a thumbs-up, my phone was dark. Too much like my mood, so I got moving.

I was on the road in my truck before I knew what I'd do. The trail disappeared in many spots where hiker-trodden leaves hid rocks and dirt. Their brown surface glistened with the morning frost's sugar-coating wherever the sun streamed through bare trees.

Relieved to be outdoors where my mental state could recalibrate, I positioned my red college toboggan over my ears. Forty degrees in the woods offered me the brisk distraction I needed. I quickened my pace to get a sweat worked up. The slick floor kept my focus off the Angie problem for a while.

When I reached the spot on the trail where I'd confessed about my long-ago engagement, I paused. Picturing Angie with her head down over the shoe she'd been tying reminded me of her surprising reaction. But should I have been surprised? That woman, gorgeous though she was, presented as a wound-up mess.

In a house of brothers, we experienced the masculine drama of yelling, arm wrestling, and the occasional chokehold. Angie's anxious reactions that I witnessed had introduced me to a powerful emotional view of the world.

Yet... had I truly appreciated how all that affected Angie's approach to life?

A cracking twig made me spin around to see a mountain bike rolling up the path behind me. I stepped aside and said, "Good morning."

The guy in black and bright yellow biking gear held up a hand in reply. I pondered his bare calves as he rode in the direction I too was headed. A different breed, I chuckled.

Such differences I always readily considered, but I hadn't done so for Angie, I concluded. I'd been a jerk last night by denying I'd done anything wrong. That was my opinion. Not Angie's.

I hustled back to my truck, working up a sweat that required undressing down to shirt and pants when I got there.

I had no idea what I needed to do, and waiting didn't feel like the right solution. But what choice had Angie given me?

Chapter 18

Angie

I RESENTED HAVING TO behave, but adult Angie possessed a more compliant attitude than my sixteen-year-old self ever had. Early Friday morning, with only fifteen days till the wedding, Carolyn Johnson in the city office helped me relax while I completed the renovation application, an ancient legal requirement to prevent people from ruining anything of historical significance. Something that made me scoff inside since no one in the city had ever shown any interest in that block, at least in my memory.

The original use of that building remained a mystery, though they'd had at least ten days to comb city records after Brian's fateful call. I'd like to choke the man for pulling me away from the store and the venue project. Sleepless nights had not helped the situation.

Bottom line, the space possessed many chapel-like features like stained glass, chandeliers, and detailed paneling. John, on his initial visit weeks ago, pointed out that the floors bore no marks from church pews or chair legs. Strange indeed.

What it had once been didn't matter much to me unless I decided to go into the venue business. But I knew marketing would necessitate "the story" of the space. The space had to serve as a chapel for Sylvie and Pete. Not that they'd approved of this idea yet. It remained my secret. My secret weapon, as I'd begun to call it.

I'd pushed Dad to the wall, working on his better nature to help a family friend. His agreement had loads of contingencies. Hearing him say "if" a million times had left me crippled with more doubt. Was it possible I could doubt myself any more after Brian betrayed my trust?

Mom politely listened, not wanting to take sides, which ticked me off, to be honest. However, she helped me a lot. Not offering praise or criticism, she allowed me to work through the issues. And boy were there issues. Sadly, some might be costly.

The heating and air conditioning company would arrive between eleven and two that same day, and I prayed the two units I wanted addressed hadn't gone completely dead. Please God, cut me a break, I whispered almost hourly. I'd been asking for a lot lately — mercies of timing, extra mercies of low expenses.

With Sunday, December twenty-second looming large on the calendar, worrying about heating and plumbing costs pushed my anxious head to its limit. Because Dad had expressed so many doubts and offered no help, I'd been forced to dig into my moving out savings to make this happen.

Proving everyone wrong — my parents, Brian, even Vanessa, who'd raised her thick black eyebrows — had become my reason for being. The Christmas season could go straight to you-know-where while I focused on this ill-conceived endeavor.

As I pulled into the mercantile parking lot, Sylvie's text jarred me out of my spinning thoughts.

Update?

Her pointed word was at least accompanied by a heart emoji, the deep red one, my favorite. I loved it more than the double pink hearts. She's pressing her knee into my back alongside a reminder of our deep friendship.

I sighed as I began typing.
Can I show you something? Open mind required.
You promised me pictures days ago!
Hang on. I'll call you when I get inside.
ok
I need a few minutes.
Ohhh-kay
Gotta love her sarcasm. And her patience under these awful bridal circumstances.

"Vanessa, I'm so sorry."

"For what? It's all good."

"Is it though? I've dumped the store operations on you all week. When did you go home last night?"

She waved me away. "It's Christmas, sweetie. One does what one must."

"But it's been so busy and I'm absent! I'm sorry we don't have more staff. I've tried... but..."

"Your dad. I get it. I've avoided calling our Mr. Caruso to the floor. He gets flustered sometimes. Can I be honest? I mean, the timing's not good—"

"Oh lord, you're not leaving me. Please, no."

"I was going to say... I wish we were even busier, considering the season. And don't you fret about me leaving cuz I'd never leave the best boss I've ever had."

I seldom think of myself as the boss, only when I am making the occasional "permitted" decision about the store. Vanessa feels like a partner, not an employee. But I had too much else to do to get into all that with her then, though I probably should make the time.

"You're the best, you know that? And..."

"And what?"

"I need to go to the new space for a little while."

Vanessa shrugged as she hung ornaments on a tree to replace those sold. Why people didn't take them out of the baskets underneath, I'd never understand.

"Seriously, I shouldn't be more than thirty minutes." I looked at my phone. "Can you call in a lunch order for you, Dad, and me from Parkside Cafe down the street? Tell them to put it on my bill. If that confuses them, tell them to ask Lisa. She knows me. Thanks."

"Done. Now go do your wedding thing." She wiggled her fingers to wave me off.

I tossed my coat and purse on my desk and hustled through the stockroom doors. Dad was on the phone, his aggravation clear by how slowly he spoke, as if to an idiot. Must be a vendor.

I flipped the lights on in the hallway, the chapel space, and all the other storefronts down the hall. I'd swept away the cobwebs from the ceiling vents the last time I passed through there.

Yesterday, I'd borrowed some folding chairs from a neighboring shop. I included them with the few we owned to create a front row with five chairs on either side of a center aisle. Sylvie's never had the design eye that I have. For interiors anyway. Her gardening eye boggled my mind, which I was reminded of when I saw the flowers she'd chosen for the wedding. I just wasn't sure if she would picture the space as a chapel if I didn't create the image for her.

She picked up immediately after I hit the call button. "Show me."

"I will, but first let me explain before I show."

The bride sighed almost hard enough to make my phone shake.

I explained everything about the space—its location and condition and my ideas for getting the entire wedding event within the rooms on our block. She murmured something about her mother's opinion.

"It's your wedding, Sylvie. And options are... truthfully... non-existent."

"You'll show her today?"

"I'll call her right after we hang up. Promise."

"Then she and I can talk, I guess."

"Perfect."

"I really do appreciate you pulling this off."

"Um, well, don't forget, I need a couple of inspections. Then there's the HVAC, sprinklers, plumbing. The electricity all seems to be in working order. A blessing I'll take."

"Ugh. Right." Sylvie sighed heavily again. Nothing was sorted out yet. I may be as stressed as the bride at this point, but I'd never say that. After the event we'll laugh about it, I hoped. But we're just not at the joking stage yet.

"Remind me of the final head count?"

"Seventy."

I didn't realize I'd been holding my breath until a gasp of relief escaped my lips.

"Oh, thank heavens. We now have options."

"We do?"

"Patience, friend. You've seen the chapel space. What do you think?"

"Um, it'll work. I mean, I trust you. Show me where Pete and I stand again?"

I turned the video on again and talked through my idea of a dark wood arch trimmed with holiday greens only. "You're gonna save your folks money on this deal. My job talking to the very particular Mrs. Bradley may actually be easy!"

"Not so fast, Ang. We're talking 'bout my momma."

"Your approval will carry weight, won't it?"

"We'll see."

"Let me show you the changing rooms and the hallway."

"Hey Ang, I'm sorry to be a Debbie-downer. I'm trying to keep myself grounded, you know, in case things go off the rails. Again."

"No worries. Okay, here are two small shop spaces across the hallway from each other. These can be changing rooms. Oh, and I'm going to get artwork and wreaths onto these hallway walls to dress it up. It's such a long dull space."

"Whatever you have time for. I'm being such a burden."

"I'm your maid of honor. And apparently wedding director too!"

We chuckled in unison.

"Angie, we haven't talked about the reception yet. Please tell me you have that covered. Momma and Constance Miller have come up empty on that front."

"I have a plan."

"Okay."

Did I hear doubt in her voice? I mentally kicked myself for keeping all this under wraps. But what choice did I have? And now, with the new wrinkle caused by that insufferable Brian's meddling, all of it might disintegrate between my fingers.

"Listen, I'm sorry I've kept you in the dark about all this. I had to get it worked out with my dad first, then the city showed up. I couldn't get your hopes up. And I may still be doing so. Everybody better put on their prayer shawls and ask for miracles."

"It's okay. I understand, I promise."

"Let me show you the kitchen I found here. It looks like it might have been a small food place, maybe an ice cream shop. No ovens, but lots of work area for a caterer."

"But who—"

"I'm getting there. Let me show you the other side. I'd thought about using it for the reception but—"

"The mystery is killing me."

Honestly, I should be thankful that Sylvie was actually grounded — more grounded than she gave herself credit for earlier. But this experience took me way out of my comfort zone, and she hadn't given me all the positive vibes I needed. Her doubt meshed with my own created a heartbeat like the pounding of horses' hooves. Would I survive this month? I wasn't certain... way too much hung in the balance. Too much to list now, but I would list it for Sylvie after I showed her the catering room. A final dose of reality before her momma got pulled in.

I did not know what I was doing. That had been made clear by my dad and by Brian. Why couldn't he mind his own business?

When I'd told him we needed a break from each other, what had I meant? I wasn't sure, and that problem was shoved to the proverbial back burner so this project could get cooking. I didn't enjoy being on a break, though. I missed talking to him and getting his cute text messages.

"I'm sending you the proposed menu from the cafe up the street. She tried to mimic some of the items on your original menu, but honestly, it isn't even close," I admitted after I'd shared a video of the final area of space with my suggestions for how to use it for the reception.

"Okay, but first I have a question that I'd like you to run by Momma. Is it possible to use the chapel space for the reception, too? I mean, it's so beautiful and warm. Elegant. The restaurant is all white and cold feeling with all that glass."

"I totally agree that the chapel space is much more intimate. Just some logistical stuff after the ceremony I need to work through. Can you give this some thought? We're gonna need a little labor from the guests. Know what I mean?"

Sylvie sighed. "I guess. Ugh, I dunno. Talk to Momma."
"So..."

"Yes. Move forward on this. Can you send pictures so I can show Pete? He's okay with anything at this point. He's just not stressing about it like I am."

"More prayer needed!"

Sylvie chuckled with me. It was not funny, however. The weight of her "yes" made my head hurt. My breathing stuttered.

"Deep breath, Ang."

"I better run, my friend. Calling your momma when I get into my office."

"K. My thanks aren't enough, of course."

"You'd do the same for me." I believed that was true, but a speckle of doubt glimmered at the corner of my eye. I'd shifted into such a negative mood about my self-worth, I couldn't even accept the words of my best friend.

"Bye, sweetie."

"Bye," I whispered, not noticing that I'd spoken after I'd hung up. I was desperate to get Momma Bradley over here, but I needed to eat before I tried to win her over to this desperate plan.

My office smelled like a buttery croissant with notes of ham. Bless Vanessa! I found her near the door straightening a wreath.

"Hey, thanks for getting the lunch ordered. I'm, uh, gonna call Sylvie's mom in a minute and hope she'll get over here today."

"Fair warning," Vanessa said with a wink. Momma Bradley could be a lot, if you know what I mean.

With my tendency toward being a Nervous Nellie, I wondered if anyone in my circle considered that I, too, was a lot. My first anxiety attack in front of Brian had unnerved him a little, at least as I remember it. He'd since fallen into a groove whenever I got shaky, which honestly hadn't happened but a few times.

I am not "a lot," I concluded as I unwrapped my sandwich and bit into it. In the quiet, I turned off my planning brain and reflected again about what I said to Brian. Maybe I had been too vague even for myself, but when I told him the other night, I was too angry to deal with him and his... handsome face. I groaned at my stupidity. I liked him far too much to give him up, but I'd done it, anyway.

"It is what it is," I muttered to myself as I dialed Sylvie's mom. I had too many pressing issues to spend any more time on the burdens of my heart.

Mrs. Bradley turned in circles, taking in the chapel space later. She'd come so late, I feared that she'd either not show up at all or I'd be at the mercantile well past dinnertime. I texted my mom to save me a plate, just in case.

"And you say it's getting a good scrub?"

"Tomorrow. A crew is coming. I'm actually thinking we might hire them to move chairs and set up for the reception in here. I may ask the cafe owner—that is, if you and Sylvie approve her menu—to use the young men to help with serving. Except for the alcohol. They're too young."

Her sigh ratcheted up my nerves—my cheeks sizzled and my fingers burned.

"We'll hire a bartender. What if the bar went in that corner, the DJ over there?"

I almost passed out from relief. She'd bought it hook, line, and sinker.

"Whatever you want. But—"

"We cannot have buts, not this late," she said while she ran her hand over the wall paneling again.

"Well, Mrs. Bradley, I still have to get this through the city's building code office."

She tapped her lips, a matte rosy pink from a seriously old cosmetic company. Yeah, I could name the high-end department store brand based on a quick glance.

"Mr. Bradley might smooth the way. God knows, he needs to do something to help with this cursed project."

Cursed?

"It's definitely been a mess, I agree. Lemme show you the rest of the building. I'll tell you everything I told Sylvie, and then we can discuss your preferences. Is that okay?"

I just wanted her quiet for a little while so I could do a big picture explanation. I was not going to discuss the stinky bathroom or why the plumber didn't show up the day before.

"It's actually toasty back here. The heating works?"

"Yep, they tuned it up earlier today. There's still the sprinkler system to install in the chapel. Thankfully, the previous owner had the foresight to outfit the rest of it before Dad bought the block."

I started walking faster down the hall, irritated with my stupid self for entering the weeds I'd wanted to avoid.

"Sounds like you've worked through everything."

I shook my head. "That's why you're here — to make sure I haven't forgotten a thing. I'd like to be a team on this, naturally. I know zilch about throwing a wedding."

"So far, dah-ling, not bad. A compromise to be sure, but that's not your fault."

Hardly high praise, but what did I expect? What a horrible position for the Bradleys. No doubt, they'd had grand plans to impress their friends at The Main with its fancy food and the shimmering chrome and glass building design.

"At least the DJ is still on. He is, isn't he?"

She nodded while she ran a finger down the long kitchen counter. Thank goodness.

"Well, he needs to contact me and check the setup here since it's way different."

"Way different, indeed," Sylvie's momma said with an eyebrow cocked at me. Ouch.

"Um, I need to get to work on some things, Mrs. Bradley. How 'bout you visit Lisa, the cafe manager, and talk to her about the reception menu?"

She looked at me like I'd asked her to eat manure. This was not happening. Was I the only person invested in Sylvie's wedding?

I stared her down until she relented with a slight nod.

"I'd have something to share with Sylvie tonight. Point me in the direction."

I unlocked the door and walked her out of the darkened store. "It's just a short one-block walk that way. Please have Sylvie call me when she can, to confirm we're on track to proceed."

"Proceed? Oh, it's a go, my dear. Let me know what else I can do. I feel a bit useless these days."

"Confirm everything? Florist, DJ, food. Hire the bartender. Oh, and ask Lisa to set up an account for you. To bill you for the reception, okay?"

"Right," she said as she pulled on tan leather gloves which perfectly matched her camel-hair coat. Vintage, of course. I swear she'd live back in the sixties or seventies if she could—and totally fit in.

"And if you think of anything, anything at all, please call or come by. I'll be here working this weekend. Okay?"

"Fifteen days. Can we do this?"

I shrugged. "Gotta do what we gotta do."

Mrs. Bradley patted my cheek with a gloved hand. "Good night, sweet girl. Get some rest."

Right.

Chapter 19

Brian

Am I an insensitive jerk? Isn't it Angie's responsibility to manage her own feelings, especially when they're so out of line? Why should I apologize?

As days flew by without hearing from Angie, I vacillated between being sorry and being furious. With only my tortured thoughts and no helpful feedback from Angie, I was winging life. And failing miserably.

Most days, I couldn't even get over her accusation. I hadn't meant to hurt Angie when I made that call, but she'd interpreted my action as a personal affront, like a reflection of my opinion of her professional capabilities. Why was her interpretation my fault — and why did she drop me like a nuisance?

I guessed I might work my way to an apology once I figured out the true wrong I'd committed.

Would she ever give me the chance to explain? Should I move on and forget everything? Forget her? Was that what she'd meant when she asked for a break? So many questions. I needed Angie to answer them, but she wasn't talking to me.

But I couldn't forget her. She'd lit up my days like no other woman had ever done. I was coming apart at the seams, and I didn't enjoy feeling like I was completely losing it. Going through the motions of life made the days go by so slowly. Maybe if time slowed down enough, Angie would have time to come to her senses.

The other part confused me. How'd she go from nearly spending the night with me to we're not right for each other? I played back what she said. Not this, not that, not enough. But she didn't understand that I believed she was more. Far more than anything I deserved. Clearly.

"It's Christmas, for heaven's sake," I whispered toward my ceiling. The moon cast a shaft of brilliant silver light on my bed. Its movement across the covers had been cataloged in my brain over the past few lonely nights when I'd savored every moment of Angie time I'd experienced.

The moon's brightness distracted me from much-needed sleep, tempting me to get up and slide the curtain over a bit. Not all the way, cuz I like the sun shining on me in the morning. For some masochistic reason, I didn't wish to interrupt my bedtime misery—the stillness of my body and the quiet rushing of my heartbeat reminded me how much I missed Angie's latent energy. When we were together, she'd sizzled across my skin, but her effect on me had gone unappreciated until she was gone.

John was my only source of information about Angie's activities. Framed, unfortunately, around all the wedding preparations. John knew nothing of my supposedly egregious error of asking a simple question of the city.

After he'd spent the entire weekend in Birmingham, away from his patient wife and Christmas-crazy kids, I peppered him with so many texts, he called me Monday night.

"Dude, what's going on?"

"It's, um, well—"

"You didn't come by this weekend. Now I get it. Are ya'll not together?"

I ran a hand over my face, pacing in front of the sofa. Emotion strangled my throat, so I stayed silent. My big brother shouldn't see or hear that I wasn't okay. No way would I let on how messed up this all was. We were well past the teenager's teasing that had sometimes bordered on bullying, but such embarrassment never goes away.

"Uh, yeah, she needed a break."

"From you?" He scoffed. I imagined him scratching his bearded jaw. "But... but you're the dream catch!"

"Apparently not right now. Listen, we can get into that later. I'm gonna get her back, you'll see," I said with false bravado.

"There's my confident bro."

"Just update me on the chapel stuff. I mean... please."

"Sure, sure. We got lots done. Those young men took to the work, not that it's that hard. But listen, the real story is the bride showed up."

"She did? Wow." I wondered if that was a relief to Angie or not.

"Yeah, I took it as a surprise. She just showed up and some squealing and hugging ensued. The usual girl stuff. She seemed nice. They hung wreaths and artwork in the hallway. Looked good."

"So you talked to Angie then?"

"Bro, you gotta fix this. I'm no messenger."

"No, I don't want that. How did she seem, though?"

"Okay, I guess. Her dad's pretty cool."

Well, that was a relief. Angie let his concerns get to her, taking them much too personally, in my opinion. At least he now sounded supportive of the project, and surely that helped Angie work through the building issues.

"What about the city involvement?"

"What's the city got to do with it?"

"Angie didn't mention it to you?"

Muffled voices told me that John had covered the phone to have a conversation with his wife, a reminder that I'd taken him away from what was far more important—his young family.

"John, I'll let ya go. Thanks for everything, man. Tell Beth and the kids 'hey' from me."

"No prob. I'll send some pics before I read to the brats." Squealing in the background brought a chuckle to my lips, a rare occurrence over the past few days.

While I popped the cap off a beer bottle, I thought about how much I'd like to read to kids at bedtime one day. Sooner rather than later. Did Angie want kids? As an only child, she may have a different perspective. Maybe she'd want a bunch, though. I'd go for that—an idea that brought a spread of warmth across my chest.

After four sips of beer, Angie and I were married with two toddlers, and all was well in my world. Those imaginative thoughts got canceled by the chime of John's text containing pictures of the gleaming chapel woodwork and teenagers hard at work.

Another message had photos of the hallway. In one, I saw Angie and Sylvie at the far end—Sylvie with lighter hair and at least a head taller than Angie. Zooming in, I read nothing in Angie's expression other than smiling at her friend.

"My guys and I will finish the chapel this Saturday. She ordered chairs and we'll set them up." John said in his last text of the night. I knew that wasn't the end of the work there, though. Next Saturday was the day before the wedding. The idea of it made my heart flutter. How was Angie getting it all done? By herself? With a scattered, emotional bride at her side?

When Angie and I investigated the space and I'd encouraged her to pursue its use, my visions included me wielding a hammer or a mop. The photos of the beautiful building and the one of Angie left me empty. Missing this transformation was never part of my plans.

I was ready for a long-term commitment with Angie, but she must have other ideas. My confident declaration to John was a figment of the overactive imagination of a teenager in love.

In love? Well... there's another idea. My heart stuttered wildly when I realized no matter how irritated I'd been with Angie, I had missed her with every piece of me. I didn't want to stay lost like that any longer.

The bigger question was how I could translate these deep feelings into an actionable plan—a puzzle too daunting for my engineer's brain.

Chapter 20

Angie

Sylvie called me later the next day after her momma endorsed the plan, unstable as it was. I'd stayed awake later than usual the night before, hoping to have a full discussion about her concerns and such. I fell asleep with my phone in hand, unplugged all night and dead when I woke to warm sun on my face.

The store had been busy, tearing me in half between helping customers and advising John's work team. He easily managed the small repairs, plus the basic cleaning and polishing needed. But he had a few questions like future placement of the sprinkler system—gosh, I wish I'd avoided all that. Thanks, Brian, I muttered under my breath now and then.

John called a plumber friend who lived between Tuscaloosa and Birmingham, extracting a promise to come in a day or two. In the meantime, my plan included giving a deep scrub to that hallway bathroom and the two tiny ones over in the restaurant area which were already marked by his and hers signs.

Sylvie and I were chatting about the menu, which her momma had amended a little. Lisa's pretty amazing and I suspected we'd become friends. I loved her food. Standing in the open doorway of the chapel, I let the frigid fresh air inside. Sylvie's voice sounded strange, like an echo over the phone.

"You sound strange," I said.

"I sound close. Turn around."

I turned and instantly squealed, running into her open arms. All the stress of this wedding, this stupidly stressful event, melted away. Her red wool coat scratched my cheek, but I didn't care as I drank in the light floral scent she always wore. Her hair smelled a little like bananas reminding me of our seventh-grade selves.

"Oh gosh, lemme hang up the phone."

"This is so beautiful! Your videos didn't do it justice."

"Admit it, you were worried as heck."

Sylvie nodded. "But I trusted you. I'm overwhelmed by what you've accomplished."

I hugged her again and pulled her out of the chapel and away from the teenage boys' curious stares. I'd introduce her to John later.

Slipping my arm into hers, I dragged her down the hall, chattering away about what needed doing still.

"I'm here to help."

"But what about work? Did you ditch Patrick for the rest of the month?"

"He'll be getting used to that."

"You're still quitting then," I said, a note of doubt about this decision crept into my tone. I didn't believe that my best friend required my approval, but she surely suspected I wondered if leaving her job was the right thing to do.

"Actually... no."

I swung around to look at her face, wondering what more news I could take in one day.

She smiled and said, "I'm gonna be part time when we get back from Costa Rica. And I'll be working a little this week cuz I need to interview some internship candidates. We've already found office space in a growing area in the city, not too far from the university."

"That sounds awesome. I'm so happy for you, you know. Let's sit here for a minute." I gestured toward a round table with two white bistro chairs in the former restaurant space.

"What's this space for?"

"For *your* event, this'll be staging for the caterer. Oh, did your momma finish going over the menu with Lisa? I gave her that job. Gosh, I sound bossy, don't I?"

"Someone had to take control, and she was relieved to be contributing something. Finally. I think she's cried more than me. She's really proud of you, too."

"You're okay with all this?" I had to ask because she had the look of someone with no cares. Maybe I'd carried too many these past few weeks. Had I stolen part of the experience from her?

She let out a long breath, and my tummy tightened in anticipation of bad news. Or negative reviews. Then she shrugged. "It is what it is. Pete's been amazing, especially when I started bouncing off the walls a few weeks ago."

"Good, good," I said distractedly. Her mention of Pete was a knife in my gut. I missed Brian after a week of no communication. But this wedding venue had pushed me to where I just wanted the year to end and let me get on with a new focus—whatever it might be.

"Hey, sorry. I'm being selfish. Tell me about Brian. Sounds like things are moving along well."

Heart in my throat, I shook my head. "I messed that up."

"What? But his brother—"

"Doesn't know. Well, he hasn't mentioned Brian. Perhaps he does. They're close, so Brian may have told him I needed a break." I made air quotes on the last word.

"But why? Did all this Sylvie-provoked stress have anything to do with it? I'd hate to..." She stopped talking when tears dripped down my cheeks. "Aw, honey." Sylvie slid her chair closer, the scrape of the legs echoing in the empty room.

"It's okay. This distraction helps. I just got so mad at him when he called the city. It's like everyone assumes I'm stupid and destined to mess up everything."

"But look what you've done!"

"Yeah, it's actually good. And if the city gives me all the approvals I need, I might keep the venue option open."

"You should! It's just... Wow! Words escape me. Who imagined this could happen right next door to the mercantile?"

"Well, after your wedding—again assuming the city comes through—I have some convincing to do. My dad, well, he's another naysayer."

"I don't understand. He's letting my wedding go on and getting it fixed up. It has to cost something."

"I'm the one paying for the repairs." I pointed to myself with both thumbs.

"Which reminds me. Momma mentioned nothing about what you're charging to use this space. We can't just take it."

"I don't need your money. You're the guinea pigs, and so much can go wrong between now and... and the end of the wedding." I grimaced at the idea of a wedding day disaster, but we couldn't dismiss the possibility of something going sideways.

Her dark blonde hair swished as she shook her head back and forth. "Nope, nope, nope. We're paying. Consider your pricing. Now."

"I wouldn't know where to start."

"I remember what we were going to pay The Main. And Daddy made a fifty percent deposit. Returned, of course. I'll ask them about giving you that."

"Oh Sylvie, I can't take money from your family. You *are* family."

"You can and you will."

I stood up and beckoned her to the door of the restaurant. Across the street was the city park. Bare tree branches laced the icy blue sky, soft green cedars dotted the park. Holly, glossy green and dense with red berries, surrounded a gazebo constructed of natural wood.

"Good for photos, don't you agree?"

"Depending on the weather, yes. Though I saw a long-range forecast for the rest of December and it should be dry. Definitely no snow." She giggled. We bumped our elbows and laughed.

"You and your new love of snow. But you'll have to move further north to see much."

"I doubt I can tear Pete away from Richmond or Virginia, for that matter."

"But you like it there too, right?" I like Pete a lot, but I wouldn't wish for my bestie to give up a dream for any man. Me being a relationship expert and all. Haha.

"I love it there. I'd love anywhere if Pete's with me, to be honest."

"Spoken like a bride-to-be."

"It's true!"

"He's a great catch."

"So back to Brian. What're you doing about calling an end to this so-called break you've taken?"

I shrugged.

"Angela Caruso! You didn't lie during all those after-date phone calls. He's special. What if he's the one?"

"The one? Come on, Sylvie. I don't even know that myself."

"Mmm. Maybe. But he sure filled your conversations. I know your voice, my friend. Sometimes I sensed intrigue and other times you sounded wistful."

"Well, right now, I'm *wish*ful. Wishing you'd drop this topic."

"Pfft. Get him back. Before the wedding. I wanna meet this black-haired lover who got hold of your heart."

I groaned and pushed her back inside.

"I was wondering. For the outdoor photos, do you have a cape or wrap?"

"Um." Sylvie made a face.

"Your dress is so sleek. Wouldn't it look great with a white fur stole around your shoulders?"

I pulled my phone from my coat pocket and starting scrolling. I held up a screen of images of the gorgeous idea I'd just offered.

"Hmm. Pretty. I suppose it would. Or we can pray for sunshine and summer temperatures."

"Really. You mock me?" I quirked an eyebrow, playing up my annoyance with her cavalier attitude.

"Joking."

"Let's go hang stuff."

"Hey, you haven't mentioned your mom."

"Oh, poor woman has been down with the flu for almost a week. She'd planned to help with dusting baseboards and cleaning toilets, and whatever else I asked, but that's not happening. It's awful when a parent gets sick. I'm useless at helping her."

I thought about our interaction that morning when I checked in on Mom from the doorway, covers pulled up to her chin. A space heater hummed near the end of the bed.

"Morning, Mom. Can I get you another cup of tea before I go?"

She shook her head, making her salt-and-pepper hair spread in a fan on her pillow. "I'm okay," she said with a rasp. She started to say something else, but a fit of coughing rocked her.

"Should we call the doctor again? Are you finished with the prescription she gave you?"

She nodded her head, then shook it. "No call, yes done," was all the effort she mustered.

Tears pricked the corners of my eyes. I hated to see this woman who usually had Christmas prep well in hand by now suffering. Only our tree was up. I'd remembered to hang her favorite wreath on the front door last night—determined to contribute something at home before I fell exhausted into bed.

I walked into the room, hoping not to catch anything, to feel her forehead with the back of my fingers. "You don't feel feverish. You sure you don't want anything?"

"Sleep."

"Perfect. You do that. Lots of rest, you hear? Oh, you wanted an update on the wedding stuff. It's going great, surprisingly so."

"Of course it is, my angel. You're so talented," she whispered as her voice broke into another cough.

My face grew warm. I didn't know how to react to her praise. Not after all the doubt that'd been whispering in my head. My heart wasn't doing so great either. "Just get better so you can see it on the wedding day. And say a prayer. Or two. Or three. Please?"

She waved a hand at me as I closed the door to the bedroom she and my dad had shared since I was a baby.

"Do you need to check on your mom? I can wait in your office."

"She's good. I called her at lunch." I looked at my phone for the time. "Gosh, Dad'll be leaving soon. We gotta work."

"Dad," I called out in the stockroom. I wondered where he'd gotten to. This place had kept him on his toes all month. Please, Otis, get back soon.

We found him near the door with Vanessa and Carolyn Johnson—the city lady, as I'd continued to call her. Vanessa held a manila folder in one hand, her other covered her mouth, so I naturally concluded we had a problem. Dad was asking a question. I scurried ahead of Sylvie, eager to get the lowdown, regardless of how bad it might be. I had to hear what obstacle I needed to overcome. How much more bad news could Sylvie handle?

"There's nothing we can do about that? In this short time?"

We? Dad said "we." What?

"Good day, Miss Caruso. Just delivering your renovation approvals."

"But what was my dad asking you?"

"Um, well, it's nothing you need to worry about for this event. A wedding, right?"

"Yes. This is the bride. Sylvie Bradley." Sylvie stepped forward to shake her hand.

"Miss Bradley, a pleasure. Your father is a delightful man."

Sylvie's mouth opened and shut. Then she kept it that way. Knowing so much about her frustrations with her daddy, I understood the decision to say nothing.

"So, not to get in the weeds so late in the day, but what would we have to do after? Like, if we keep using the space." I kept my eyes on Ms. Johnson, even though Dad's eyes bore into the side of my head.

"Just a full inspection. Safety is the greatest concern for any venue. The new sprinklers passed the basic test, but a thorough review is needed."

I frowned. "You tested them?"

"Mm-hmm, my inspector ran the test a few minutes ago."

Oh goodness, I should be thankful Sylvie showed up to distract me. I escaped a major anxious moment while we checked out the park.

"We can hold the wedding here. Is that what you're saying?" My heart pounded so hard I was certain everyone heard it.

"Yes."

"In six days? You don't need to see anything else before that?"

Ms. Johnson wrapped a tan and black plaid scarf around her neck and said, "I will see you when you call me for a final inspection. In the new year, I hope? This area of the city could use this kind of business."

My knees went rubbery. I wanted to pass out from relief. "Yes, I promise. And thank you so much."

"Merry Christmas to the Mercantile from the City of Birmingham." She walked through the door my very serious-looking dad held open for her. "Oh, one more thing."

"Yes?" I squeaked.

"Signage for that hallway bathroom is required. Paper is fine. For now, anyway."

"Okay." I'd already planned to do that, and my self-esteem took a hit for not getting the task completed by the time she came back. But I hadn't known when the city lady was coming—my rational side put up its defense.

As the door closed, a collective sigh of relief whooshed through the store. We were about to close for the night, since no customers wandered amongst the displays. "Jingle Bells" played over the speakers, a good omen for what was to come.

"Well, Ang, I'm headed home to check on Mom. Dinner ideas?"

"Um." I looked at Sylvie and we shrugged in unison. "Can Sylvie and I bring something for the three of us?"

"Sure. Don't be late. I'm hungry."

"Same," I said as I walked with him to the stockroom for his coat.

"Angie, hon, let's get through this wedding. Okay? Hold off on future plans?"

Why did he have to be such a killjoy?

"Whatever you say," I said with a resigned sigh. I'd been avoiding him the last few days, so I didn't have to hear him say things like, "Inspections aren't scheduled overnight" and "Don't get your hopes up, Angie." I didn't need that kind of negativity infecting my erratic days.

After Dad went to the family room for some TV time, Sylvie and I finished a bottle of white wine. The pizza box between us held bits of black olive and the crusts we'd both discarded. Visions of snug fancy dresses danced in our heads.

"Angie, dear friend, we can't have you lonely with a wedding and Christmas looming only a week away."

"Sylvie, no," I whined.

"Who ended the relationship?"

Relationship? Was that what I had with Brian? We'd never said we were exclusive, had we? But I'd made him exclusive in my life. Not that I had time to dangle two—or three—guys on the line trying to decide on the best fish. What about Brian—what had he been up to?

Come on, Angie, I scolded myself. Brian told me how he felt often enough, and I dismissed him in my head and my heart. Fear had paralyzed me, though I couldn't pin down what specifically prompted me to be so terrified.

"Me. I ended it."

"What're you afraid of?" She had to ask, darn her.

"I... don't..." I couldn't finish my stupid admission, so I hung my head to avoid her gaze.

I reached in my jeans pocket for a tissue, a new accessory, since I gave Brian the boot. I'd behaved so foolishly when I blamed him for all my project's issues. I still didn't appreciate him butting in, but my refusal to listen to his explanation meant I'd failed him royally.

"Do you like him? Or have stronger feelings?"

"He didn't even try to get me back. When his engagement fell apart, he flew all the way to Kansas! It's like he took me dumping him in stride."

"Did you want him to come begging?"

"Not really." I rolled my eyes. "Kind of embarrassing, don't you think?"

"Embarrassing? What're you talking about? Think back to about this time last year and what did you do?"

"You mean when I called Pete? And, uh, lit a fire under him?"

"Yes! And here I am, your own fire starter friend." She smiled at me like she'd just said something brilliant. I suppose she had. "And you didn't answer my question about your feelings, Ang."

"Oh, that, well... I'm crazy about him."

"Surprise, surprise," Sylvie used a high-pitched southern drawl to imitate Gomer Pyle from an old show I sometimes watched as a kid. I smiled through my tears.

"What do I do now, though? I mean—"

"Call? Text? Show up on his doorstep?"

"Oh lord, I can't do that," I moaned, my head in my hands.

"Oh well," Sylvie said as she shrugged, her hands busily folding the corners of her paper napkin over and over. I expected her to ask for scissors next so she could make it into a snowflake.

I put my head down on my folded arms, the wood table a little slippery under the smooth knit of my red sweater. With my eyes closed, I listened to the sounds of the house—Dad's television show and Sylvie checking wine bottles.

"Glasses are empty, and I'm pretty sure we need more. You definitely do. Wanna try a red or stick with white?" Her emphasis on "definitely" reminded me of our high school years, when Sylvie tried her best to keep me on the straight and narrow. She never shamed me when her advice failed to reach my head or, at times, my heart.

In answer to her red or white question, I whimpered, "Don't care."

"Gotcha. What or who do you care about, Ang?"

"You."

"Girl, that I know. Your work on our wedding puts you into primo friend status. I'm so blown away."

"Thanks. A work of love, my friend." I gave her a weak smile, unable to put my aching heart into the effort.

"You're such a great friend. I can't see how you aren't a wonderful girlfriend. So much love in that big heart of yours."

I frowned, doubt weighing heavily on my thoughts. "You think so?"

"Well, not to get weird, but I can see you as a girlfriend... to someone. Like Brian? When you talked about him, he sounded so perfect for you."

"What a goofball I am."

"Not a goofball, just a scared girl. Right?"

"I invited him to your wedding as my plus-one, so I wasn't that scared."

"Well, well... better get him back quick. Based on that calendar on the fridge, you got six days."

"Ugh," I moaned again as I picked up my cellphone. "Here goes nothin'."

"It's not nothin'."

I looked up from my phone. "What should I say?"

Sylvie stood and walked toward the bathroom. "That's easy. 'I'm sorry' is usually the perfect start."

Chapter 21

Brian

CAN WE TALK?

Angie had sent the simple question the night before, but I'd gone to bed early, at a loss for something to do and no one to talk to. Besides, I'd gone hiking alone and stayed out in the torturous cold for four hours. Wiped out, the blessed exhaustion pushed me into sleep and out of my blue mood.

Once I got my usual two coffees in me, I would head to the regular Sunday hike with Mike and the gang. Angie hadn't been there for a couple of weeks, and curiosity might rear its ugly head.

My curiosity, though, was piqued. Was Angie ready to hash out what was going on between us? Was I?

Her rejection still stung. I'd been so invested in getting to know her the past two months, after finding myself instantly attracted. A vision of her smile when she entered the restaurant that first evening tugged at my heart. Smiling at me — a virtual stranger — across the heads of diners, Angie revealed her warmth and tender spirit.

She'd been a dream girl from the start until the nightmare of her pushing away ruined the holiday season, and everything else.

I should've been glad she wanted to talk, but doubt plagued me. How much fight did I have left to keep her in my life? Or — the idea buoyed me — maybe Angie planned to apologize and pull me back into her orbit.

I shoved the phone into my puffy jacket and headed for the hike. Brisk air and the crunch of rocks under my boots would clear my head. Let's be serious here—I hadn't had good judgment since meeting that little dynamo. Time for a more rational Brian to return to the scene, but I let her text message hang out there for a little longer.

Passive-aggressive? Probably, yeah. I didn't enjoy doing it, but I needed to protect my hurting heart. Part of me hated the idea of her torment as she waited for my response. She'd be certain I'd respond. Eventually.

Then again, what did she really know about me? Or I about her? We'd covered a lot of ground through personal storytelling, and there'd been an occasional surprise. I still didn't get how someone as capable as Angie allowed others so easily dash her confidence to the ground.

My parents had always been the most encouraging people, and I took their ongoing approval for granted. While Angie's father seemed pretty cool overall, he didn't give Angie's skills enough credit based on the stories she'd shared with me.

She'd had a lot going on since I met her and handled it amazingly well. She needed to establish her capable spirit in her dad's mind and her own. There I was... thinking about squeezing her heart in my hands, making her wait for me to respond. What was wrong with me?

After my post-hike shower and protein drink, I responded to Angie.

Happy to talk. What'd you have in mind?

A few minutes passed before the three dots danced on the screen. I had to take a few deep breaths to relax the muscles in my chest while I waited. Was she writing a novel?

I'm not sure, really. Can I see you in person?

I've got a work party tonight.

I'd planned to invite Angie to attend, but she'd stuck a knife in that opportunity.

Dinner one night this week? Please?

Her pleading gave me brief pleasure. Not proud of that.

I'm going to the Wheeler plant to cover for their chief engineer this week. Staying overnight. Not home till Friday night.

Oh, okay.

How about Saturday?

That's the rehearsal dinner. Wedding is Sunday.

This wasn't working. I tossed caution out and posed the looming question.

Am I still invited?

Three dots appeared, then vanished.

Is that how we want to do this?

Do what, Angie?

I had to push back since she was in the driver's seat. Why did she make me feel as though I'd messed up her make-up plan? If that was what was going on.

I'm sorry.

I tossed the phone on the bed and grunted into the silence of my bedroom. What was she sorry for — the direction of this conversation or kicking me to the curb? Having no response to her tepid apology, I grabbed my black suit from the closet. None of my ties had a holiday vibe, but I found one with a little red stripe in the pattern. It'd have to do.

While I shaved, the phone buzzed again.

You still there? I AM truly sorry. I messed up big time. Come to the wedding. It's at two. Sunday.

I'll be there.

I clicked on a heart but deleted it before sending my reply. This was the strangest way to approach a breakup. And maybe a makeup.

Angie replied with a heart-eyes face.

I wouldn't be much fun at the company Christmas party, but showing up was required. Luckily, my travel early the next morning gave me the perfect excuse to slip out before drunken toasts by the managers made someone uncomfortable.

The week at Wheeler proved stressful and lonely. I didn't have time to linger on thoughts of Angie during the day. Nights were a different story. Alone in a little town, I ate at local restaurants, impressed by the signed photos of the NFL players it had produced. I'd gotten bored scrolling through the hotel's television guide, so one night I ventured into a men's store. My wedding wardrobe needed a fix, so I bought a green silk tie and a new white shirt. The shirt was folded in cellophane meaning the iron and ironing board would have to come out of storage in the back of my closet.

Why had Angie brought on this tumult of emotion now? Where had her sudden change of heart come from? Perhaps the bride had something to do with it.

I'd agreed to go to the wedding, no matter how uncomfortable it might be. The uncertainty of a reunion with Angie was enough to make me want to back out. Was I an idiot to believe a face-to-face explanation by Angie would work at an intense wedding?

Had Angie's parents heard about our breakup? Honestly, I couldn't worry about what anybody else believed. This was between me and Angie.

The transformation of the old rooms intrigued me almost as much as seeing Angie again. Curiosity about the work Angie'd accomplished lurked within the spaces not filled by images of her lovely face.

While Angie owed me something when she stood before me, I also owed my own apology for ever causing her to doubt herself. She was obviously capable of anything she put her mind to. I should've been more sensitive and less of a jerk who always had confidence to spare.

I hadn't been helpful to Angie. I'd hurt her in the worst way. And though I had so many questions about our future together, I still craved her in my life.

And that craving found me driving past the mercantile on Friday afternoon on my way home from Wheeler. It wasn't on the way at all. Far out of the way, to be honest. Why I expected to see her through a display window or find her standing on the street is beyond me. Call me nuts. As it was close to dinner, I considered parking myself at the same bar down the street. The temptation to text her would be too strong, so I placed a takeout order for my favorite beef-and-broccoli from a place near my condo. Doing my best sad bachelor impression, I let my washer run while I ate my dinner.

Two more sleeps until the wedding reunion with Angie.

Chapter 22

Angie

"I think I'm going to be sick."

"No, no, you're not. Have a sip of water, Sylvie. You'll be okay."

"Are the flowers here yet?"

Good grief, she had to ask that. At one o'clock, the flowers still hadn't arrived, and my only thought was that Flo would get the delivery done after she'd returned from church services. This was one issue of having a wedding on a Sunday. It's not a normal business day. I knew all too well.

"Your momma's checking with Flo," I lied. "It'll be fine, don't worry." A truthful promise, certainly. I mentally crossed my fingers.

Did everything go perfectly at any wedding? Probably not, being that humans were involved. How imperfect we are. A truth I'd come face-to-face with these past few weeks.

Distracting the bride became my mission. I helped her put on a gorgeous retro headpiece and said, "This is the most gorgeous thing ever. Because you've pulled your bangs over, look at how the netting shimmers on your forehead. It's really perfect." Sylvie had facial scars from a car accident we'd been in as teens, and she'd spent a decade covering them. Somehow, Pete had given her the confidence to quit hiding behind her hair.

I'd only been a bridesmaid once before, and all I had to do was show up with my lilac dress — it was hideous, by the way — and walk down the aisle and smile. This maid-of-honor deal was a lot more, especially when the matron-of-honor stood in the corner rocking her infant son while she stared out the window.

"Constance Miller, wouldn't you like a chair over there?" Sylvie asked her sister.

"Oh, that'd be nice," she drawled like a southern princess.

Sylvie looked pointedly at me. Oh, I'm supposed to get her a chair. Here ya go, milady, I thought, as I opened a padded folding chair near her.

Constance Miller had offered a sweet toast to the couple the night before at the rehearsal dinner—possibly her only contribution to the entire weekend. Had I seen her at all during the renovation work? Of course not, but I said nothing to Sylvie. She was basking in the joy of her upcoming nuptials, and no one could blame her given she'd seemingly won the lottery when she fell in love with the famous author, P. J. Monroe.

Pete had booked a private room at a local steakhouse where drinks flowed like the waterfall I'd seen on my last hike with Brian. Pete's mom, Anne, was totally adorable with her shimmery blonde bob and rosy cheeks. She'd given a wonderful toast that showed she loved Sylvie and had welcomed her fully into their small family.

I'd hoped to invite Brian to the rehearsal dinner, but, I'd ruined that. I kept a bright face during the evening until I got home and collapsed from exhaustion and emotional distress on top of my bedcovers.

Thoughts of a reunion with Brian chased the sheep I tried to count that night. The sleep that had arrived at about four in the morning was interrupted by my mother's knock on the door.

"It's eight, Angie. Don't you need to get moving?"

"Coming," I groaned wearily. I wanted to be back at the store, aka wedding venue, by noon. And that was cutting it close as the entire bridal party would arrive before one.

Mrs. Bradley had thoughtfully prepared refreshments for both changing areas, something I'd failed to consider. But I decided not to feel guilty about it because, good lord, hadn't I done enough? Don't get me wrong, the Bradleys had been extremely gracious and appreciative of my efforts. I should savor that and not worry about what didn't get done by little old me. My, how I've grown up, I thought proudly.

Pete and Sylvie had gushed over the chapel. I'd borrowed a wooden archway from a local store that used it in its window displays. It made the perfect focal point at the end of the aisle where the couple would stand. The day before, Flo had left the flower shop in the hands of her sixteen-year-old granddaughter to cover the arch with greenery. Soft sweeps of cedar punctuated by the glossy dark green of sprigs of holly.

"I'm sorry there are no berries on that holly," she'd said.

"Actually, I'd pictured it with only green, so it's perfect. Plenty of red elsewhere in here. Thank you for doing this today. I know you gotta be busy. We have had a late rush in the store."

"And here you are, little girl. Being such a good friend."

I blushed at that, a little tearful from all the emotions of the past few days, weeks, even.

"Thank you for sayin' that."

"Momma! The flowers? Are they here?" Sylvie's anxious voice jolted me out of yesterday's memory and back to wedding day reality.

Mrs. Bradley clasped her hands together and said Flo had just arrived. Mr. Bradley had volunteered to help set up the chapel and he would bring the bouquets and boutonnieres back shortly.

I watched Sylvie process what her momma had said. She wanted to see her bouquet right away.

I slipped on my silver pumps, so stunning that I swore I'd wear them again. "I'll be right back," I said as I held up my dress skirt and dashed out of the room, heels clicking on the tile floor. If Sylvie wanted to see her bouquet, I'd get it in her hands.

Unprepared to see the sun glistening through the red-and-gold glass onto the red carpet runner, I nearly stopped breathing. The chapel looked so ethereal, I half expected to hear angels singing. Everything sparkled, and soon the glass lanterns placed at the end of every other row would sparkle with candlelight too. A few guests were already seated, reminding me we had little time to waste before the processional.

From the white cloth-covered gift table, I grabbed the box holding our three bouquets and headed back up the hallway. Sylvie squealed when I walked through the door.

"Oh, Momma, look. Isn't it perfect? It's exactly what I wanted."

The three Bradley women huddled together, ooh-ing and ahh-ing over the flower arrangements we would soon be carrying down the aisle. I let them have their family moment and wandered down to the kitchen area where Lisa and her staff bustled. John's three teenaged helpers were donning the black kitchen jackets Lisa asked them to wear. They chatted amongst themselves, excited I'm sure to have a good-paying job on a Sunday afternoon. Right at Christmas-time must have made it all the more exhilarating.

Looking sharp in those jackets, they'd stand out well while setting up the buffet. There'd be no serving of food, a relief given they had no experience. Instead, they would remove plates and silverware from the tall cocktail tables when guests left them.

Lifting the lid on a foil container, the rich scent of braised pork reminded me I'd forgotten to eat anything that day. I must grab a cracker or two when I got back to the changing room. No one wants a member of the bridal party laid out on the chapel floor.

I'd read about that phenomenon while researching plans for this shindig. I must keep my knees loose and unlocked, otherwise I might tip right over when the blood flow stopped. Or some such thing. There's a lot for a bridesmaid to remember besides smiling and not licking off your lipstick before you walk down the aisle.

I'd more likely faint when I had to greet Brian. I still hadn't figured out what I was gonna say or how I would say it. Should I just blurt out what a total fool I had been or apologize for blaming him for my city problem? Granted, he'd ultimately saved me a couple of headaches, but he couldn't have known that when he called the city. Anyway, that's how I'd lead off my apology—by thanking him for making that fateful call.

I'd just bitten into a cracker when Sylvie's cousin Mary told us we had only ten minutes to get outside to the chapel doors. Yes, we had to go outside in December. It's a short walk though, like twenty yards on the sidewalk from the changing room. The guys had a longer walk because they weren't allowed to cut through our space. Wedding protocol about not seeing the bride being super important to Mrs. Bradley.

The bride. Well, let me tell you, she looked stunning. Even though she'd lost nearly ten pounds from the extra stress, the satin flowed beautifully over her curves. A white fur stole graced her shoulders and though she'd bought it for the outdoor walk and photos, she chose to wear it for the ceremony clasped in front with an enameled holly pin passed down from her late paternal grandmother. All I could think about was how breathtaking she'd look under the chapel chandeliers.

As she walked toward her groom, I saw her smile falter, then recover. Must be nerves, I figured, as I'd surely be a wreck on my own wedding day. It would happen for me one day too, I hoped. Of course, at that moment, movement in the back row caught my eye. Brian was scratching his nose, looking gorgeous. He looked right at me and winked. I was so relieved, but I still wasn't sure if I should giggle or cry, so I bit my lipstick-coated bottom lip and looked away.

I returned to the chapel after the photo session in the park, shivering like a scared puppy. The bride and groom and their parents remained out there, though I doubted it'd be too long before they came back inside. I entered as the young men from Tuscaloosa carried in the last of the tall cocktail tables. Rows of chairs rimmed the room, and the arch had been shifted a short way over to the right front corner where it showcased the white three-tiered wedding cake. I stopped a minute to watch the DJ setting up his equipment. A short line had already formed in front of the bartender's walnut-and-black bar.

I turned in a circle to take it all in, while guests wandered around greeting one another. Truly an intimate gathering of Pete and Sylvie's closest associates and family. Moving things around had taken a little longer than I would have liked, so if I did decide to host other weddings and events, the process needed tweaking.

"This looks fabulous, Angie," Brian's voice tickled against my neck. I turned around to face him only inches away, heart pounding so hard he could surely see the lace on my dress bodice bouncing.

As our neighbor, Mrs. Goldberg, would say, "Oy vey." Brian looked way too good for me to focus on my little speech. My gaze drifted toward his lips until I caught myself.

"Hey." I searched his face for anything to help me know where his head was. Or the condition of his heart. A blank canvas was all he offered. He was pushing me out onto a limb, it seemed.

"Can I see the rest? You've accomplished a lot in a short time." He held out an arm toward the door to the hallway. I knew he wanted to get me alone. Make me say my piece, hand him a pound of my apologetic flesh. My stomach lurched toward my hurting heart, and I felt sick myself. My nerves simmered with doubt and fear, like those of an anxious bride in a gothic novel.

I kept my eyes down as I passed him in the doorway. Ever the gentleman, Brian held the door, but he watched me intently.

As I started up the hallway, Brian touched my arm. "I can see that later. I just wanted to see you. Alone."

"I... I know," I stammered, looking everywhere but at him. "Besides, I can't leave all that in there for long." What was I saying? *I'm too busy to talk to you right now.* I wanted to scream at myself for being such an idiot.

"I'm glad to be here. I missed you."

I couldn't talk with my throat taut with emotion. Fear tingled around my pounding heart. I had so much to say, to be sorry for. No words came, so I reached up and touched his cheek. He took my hand in his and kissed my fingers. My knees threatened to give out.

"Wait. I need to say—" Why would he let me off the hook so easily? I didn't deserve such grace after the way I'd treated him.

"Angie, you don't need to do or say anything. No apology required. I think I owe you one, though."

"No," I exclaimed, shaking my head. "You did nothing wrong. I was wrong about... well, everything."

"I mean that I wish I'd told you more often how amazing you are. So smart, so determined. This place... what you've done. It sparkles just like you. Everyone surely must see your heart and soul in it."

I shook my head, tears threatening. I didn't deserve to hear Brian say all this when I was the one who should be offering my mea culpa.

Before I could respond, he whispered, "I desperately need to kiss you."

Brian leaned in as the sounds of clapping and wild catcalls reached us from the chapel. My dad stepped through the doorway, obviously looking for me.

"They're making their entrance. I'm sure you don't want to miss this."

I nodded.

Brian laced his fingers into mine. "What excellent timing your dad always has," he whispered into my hair. I blushed as I passed my dad.

"Nice to see you again, young man." Dad shook Brian's hand.

"Thank you, sir."

Pete was in the process of twirling a blushing and giggling Sylvie in the doorway. Backlit by the bright December sun that had begun its descent into late afternoon, they created a classic silhouette. This reception would go into the dark of night, no doubt. The guests were giddy, and the music amplified the party mood.

"Who knew this chapel could be party central, too?" I mused to my parents standing next to me.

"Darling girl, your father and I owe you an apology."

"You do?"

"We doubted you," my father interjected. "I hate to admit it. But... this is quite an accomplishment."

"You've done an amazing job, Angela. It's incredible."

"Thanks, Mom. And Dad."

Dad had more to say. "Ang, um, Mrs. B told us that couple — the ones at the bar over there — they asked about renting this."

My heart skipped a beat, dread filling my chest. More delaying tactics by Dad were on their way. "What did you tell her?"

"He told her to talk to you about the date!" my mom said excitedly.

"You really mean it? I can—"

"Yes, you obviously *can* do this. We're so proud of you, hon. I'm just sorry I was skeptical. And so terribly wrong."

I smiled up at Brian, who'd listened quietly to the entire exchange. He put his arm around my shoulder.

"There's more," my dad said. "The store will cover the repair bills when they arrive. You need to create a bank account for this venue. Do it however you like."

"Really? It's my project for real. I've been thinking that we, I mean 'I', can paint the hallway and—"

"She's something else, isn't she?"

My parents nodded and said in chorus, "She sure is."

"May I steal your daughter for a dance?"

They shooed us onto the dance floor, where everyone was slow dancing to the tune the couple had chosen for their first dance. I hadn't been paying very close attention to all the wedding activity since Brian touched me. Perhaps I'd finally relax. Sinatra's "All the Way" kept our movements slow and our bodies close.

"Did you pick this song? It totally sounds like you."

"Nope, but I did send Sylvie a lengthy playlist."

"In your free time, huh?"

I rolled my eyes and giggled. "Right."

"You look so beautiful, Angie."

"So do you. I mean, you're so handsome I can barely breathe. Those blue eyes, like the sky outside..." I sighed and shook my head. "Every minute with you changes me somehow. I'm different, just slightly altered, after. It took me too long to see it."

He murmured something against my ear. When he started humming, I pulled back to look at him.

"Brian... I'm sorry, really, truly sorry, for hurting you. I let my personal issues blind me."

"You gave me some time to think about us long term and...and well, how we make this work."

"You mean how you can work around all my anxiety and stupid issues?"

"There is nothing stupid about Angela Caruso, the most brilliant retailer and venue manager I've ever met."

I slapped his shoulder. "Oh you. That's a load of—"

"Careful," he chuckled, pulling me against him and gently swaying me, even though the song had changed to something more up-tempo.

"But... but," I stuttered, eager to share what was on my heart, but unable to find the right words with him so close. I desperately needed to offer the apology I'd been practicing.

Sylvie and Pete slid into view, and I motioned them over.

"Sylvie and Pete, this is Brian. He's the reason we are here right now."

"It's fantastic. We can't thank you enough," said Pete, beaming at us. Sylvie blew us a kiss as he spun her away, the white silk of her dress swirling round her feet. What a gorgeous couple they were.

"Come on, take me on that tour now?"

We gazed into each other's eyes, standing still so long other dancers bumped into us.

"K." I took his hand, unwilling to let anything or anyone get between us. He stopped beside the gift table and pulled a card from a gold-and-white-wrapped package. "What's that?"

"You haven't signed the card."

"Oh."

The catering staff zipped past us in the hallway, so we stepped into the ladies' dressing room.

"This is where we got ready." I waved my hand around the room, a lone table littered with makeup and curling irons in the corner.

Brian touched my lips with a finger. "This is where I'm going to kiss you. May I?"

Wow, he asked me for permission. I could only look deeply into his eyes and nod.

He bent his forehead to mine. "Before I kiss you, Angie. Will you promise to be my New Year's Eve date?"

"Uh, huh." I was in a weak-limbed stupor, with his warm breath on my cheek. The promise of his kiss made my heart flutter. I might have stopped breathing for an instant.

"That's wonderful to hear. We'll have to come up with—"

"Just kiss me already."

He smiled as his lips dipped to mine, then he got serious, truly serious, about kissing me.

I moaned and kissed him back. Our tongues chased each other, while Brian's hand slid down to my waist, pulling me closer. I breathed in the scent of him—a mix of wool, pine, and something sweet.

"Do I have to wait to see you again until New Year's Eve? That's like ten days away."

His eyes sparkled with something like desire or love. "Maybe we shouldn't be apart at all until then?"

I stepped back, the weight of his question pressing into my heart. Did I want to be with him? Oh yes.

"Yikes. I need to... um. Living with my parents, I'm just always there." I twisted my dress between sweaty fingers.

"Ooh-kay. Maybe it's too much to ask you to sign a gift card and come back to my place." Brian grinned, like the good sport he'd consistently been. He'd been a trooper coming alongside my craziness. And there I was, acting like a teenager, afraid of her parents.

"Well, I did promise to return to your place with more garland. You're not just angling for a home decorator, are you?"

"You think I'm just interested in your garland, Angie?"

"I'm silly, aren't I?"

"Not asking your parents' permission, then?" He chuckled in my ear as he pulled me against him. Oh, how good his strong body felt pressed against mine. Any doubts about spending the night with Brian fled as heat simmered all over my body.

I whispered against his tie. "Is it time to blow this party yet?"

Brian tossed his head back, laughing. "Nope. We have to stay the required time."

"A girl can dream, though. You certainly have filled mine every single night since we met."

"My dream girl, that's you." He kissed the top of my head, and I turned my face up to him.

"I wanna leave with you right now so bad," I whispered against his lips. "But as a venue manager, I believe I have to lock up."

"Afraid so, miss."

I pouted playfully, and Brian's response was a wiggle of his eyebrows.

"Oh boy, I'm in trouble, aren't I, mister?"

THE END

Acknowledgments

I've been reading acknowledgments pages for decades, secretly judging authors who thank their coffee shops and their cats with equal enthusiasm.

Writing a book truly takes a village, and I'm blessed with the best village people. (They know what I mean.)

First, my middle child Victoria deserves combat pay for listening to my endless plot ramblings. She's the one who gently suggests revolutionary ideas like "Maybe finish writing the current book before you start the next one?" Revolutionary, indeed. My other children politely nod when I talk about my stories, but Victoria gets the full torture treatment—I mean, the full creative process. She's basically my unpaid therapist with lovely hair.

Mom always asks how the writing is going, bless her heart. I know the moment I start explaining character arcs, her eyes glaze over, but she keeps asking anyway. That's true love, folks.

My former neighbor Amy unknowingly became my personal focus group when she had a visceral reaction to my hero's original name. I never asked what traumatic experience she'd had with a "Matt," but her horror was so genuine that I immediately crowdsourced the character-naming job to my newsletter subscribers. They embraced this responsibility with the seriousness of naming a royal baby, and "Brian" won by a landslide. Plot twist: Brian is Amy's son's name and a dear friend's husband's name. My hero definitely grew into his new identity—sometimes the crowd really does know best.

Finally, to everyone who's taken a chance on this late-blooming author: you're the real MVPs. Thank you for buying my books, recommending them to friends, and pretending not to notice when I lurk in bookstores, rearranging my covers to face forward. (Not really, but I might one day.) Your support means everything to this slightly neurotic writer who still can't believe people want to read her stories.

Now go forth and spread the word about Angie and Brian—they're counting on you!

About the author

J.J. Ranson (friends call her Julie, and after reading her work, you'll feel like one too) spent most of her working life in education. She's a voracious reader with an ability to spot brilliance within the first few pages. She felt destined to consume words, not create them.

Then something magical happened. The words that had been flowing in for decades suddenly wanted to flow out. Julie discovered that her years of devouring stories had been secretly preparing her to tell them. What she's learned from this unexpected writing life: never, ever sell yourself short.

Julie lives in Virginia near her three adult children and one granddaughter. She's also dog-mom to two rescue pups who've trained her well in treat distribution. Her other passions include knitting, cooking (where she treats recipes like writing—a little improvisation never hurt anyone), and gardening.

Julie believes in second chances, everyday magic, and that it's never too late to surprise yourself.

Subscribe to her wonderful newsletter: https://bit.ly/jjransonnews

Follow her on:
Amazon—https://bit.ly/jjransonamazon
Goodreads—https://bit.ly/jjransongoodreads

Other books by

J. J. Ranson

She Danced Anyway

She didn't break the rules. She rewrote them. Set in the smokey dance halls of 1920s NYC.

**His Christmas Muse
(Book 1 of The His & Hers Christmas series)**

He's a best-selling author. She's his unexpected muse. But can a Christmas in Richmond rewrite their story?

I don't write in the quiet. Needing a little background noise, I depend on music most of the time. While writing Her Christmas Project, I developed a playlist of songs I enjoy—music and lyrics that have meaning for me. These tunes also help tell the emotional up-and-downs of Angie and Brian's love story. I hope you enjoy my musical choices as much as I have.

Her Christmas Project playlist: https://bit.ly/hcp_playlist

The following things won't cost you a penny:
1. Request *Her Christmas Project* at your local library (so they order it!)

2. Leave a review on Goodreads and Amazon (a purchase record is not required to leave your opinion)

3. Follow me on Goodreads and Amazon author pages (find links on the "About the author" page)

4. Recommend my stories to others

5. Invite me to a group meeting

6. Like and share my book posts on social media

7. Subscribe to my newsletter bit.ly/jjransonnews

Arrabbiata Sauce Recipe

Serve with penne or similar pasta. Yields 2 cups.

<u>Ingredients</u>

- 1 large can (28 ounces) whole peeled tomatoes*

- 4 large cloves garlic, peeled but left whole

- 2 tablespoons extra-virgin olive oil

- ¼ teaspoon red pepper flakes, or 2 small red chili peppers, finely chopped

- Salt, to taste

- Optional garnish: Chopped fresh flat-leaf parsley and parmesan cheese

<u>Instructions</u>

1. In a saucepan, combine the canned tomatoes (undrained), garlic cloves, olive oil and red pepper flakes.

2. On low heat, keep it at a slow, steady simmer for about 45 minutes, stirring occasionally.

3. After taking pan off the heat, remove garlic cloves and smash them with a fork, then return garlic to sauce. If desired, blend this sauce smooth with an immersion blender.

4. Add salt to taste. For a spicier sauce, add more pepper flakes to taste.

5. Stir sauce into hot, cooked pasta. Refrigerate up

to 5 days. Freeze up to 6 months.

www.ingramcontent.com/pod-product-compliance
Lightning Source LLC
Chambersburg PA
CBHW071401100726
47908CB00004B/1056